HOW **tía Lola**

JULIA ALVAREZ

Ended Up Starting Over

HOW tía Lola
Ended Up Starting Over

JULIA ALVAREZ

ALFRED A. KNOPF
new york

THIS IS A BORZOI BOOK PUBLISHED BY ALFRED A. KNOPF

Visit us on the Web! www.randomhouse.com/kids

Educators and librarians, for a variety of teaching tools, visit us at
www.randomhouse.com/teachers

Library of Congress Cataloging-in-Publication Data available upon request.

ISBN 978-0-375-86914-3 (trade) — ISBN 978-0-375-96914-0 (lib. bdg.)
ISBN 978-0-375-89995-9 (ebook)

The text of this book is set in 13-point Bembo.

Printed in the United States of America
September 2011
10 9 8 7 6 5 4 3 2 1

First Edition

To all the wonderful nieces and nephews
who Keep us aunties and *tías*
young and sassy!

contents

chapter one

How Tía Lola Saved the Swords from Starvation

Tía Lola and the children are having an emergency meeting in the big attic room in Colonel Charlebois's house. They are all brainstorming about how the Swords are going to survive now that they have moved to Vermont.

Miguel and Juanita can't help thinking about their own move here a year and nine months ago. Their parents were separating. Miguel and Juanita were leaving all their friends and their *papi* behind in New York City to come to this strange place. But at least Mami had a job. And they didn't have to be all alone in the house while she worked long hours. A few weeks after their move, their aunt from the Dominican Republic, Tía Lola, came to visit and decided to stay.

"Don't worry, Swords," Juanita says, brandishing a pretend sword, as if she were leading a charge. Swords is a fun nickname for the Espadas, whose last name means "sword" in Spanish.

"But we haven't come up with a way to earn some money," Essie wails. She is the middle Sword, the one who is usually full of ideas *and,* her father likes to add, full of *diablitos.* Whenever Papa wants to say something rude or cussy, he says it in Spanish. Like saying *"diablitos"* makes it okay to call your daughter a little devil! "I mean, Papa hasn't found a job, and our savings aren't going to last forever. If something doesn't happen soon, we're going to starve."

"I don't want to starve," little Cari sniffles. She is the youngest of the three Espadas and scares easily.

Valentino, the Espadas' golden Lab, lifts his head and sighs worriedly. If the family is going to starve, he will be the first to feel the rationing.

"Essie, you're not being helpful," Victoria scolds. As the eldest, she is always putting out the fires her middle sister starts. It's like Essie specializes in worst-case scenarios. If she could only find a job as a worst-case scenario consultant, the family would be millionaires.

"We, your *amigos* and *amigas,* will not let you starve!" Tía Lola assures them. She nods toward Miguel and Juanita. "And remember, your friend Rudy will always welcome you at his restaurant." Rudy owns the wildly popular Amigos Café in town. Tía Lola has helped out so many times on busy nights, Rudy has said that whenever she or her friends want a meal, it's on the house.

But Victoria knows her father would never accept a free meal. "Papa would think it was charity."

"So we go by ourselves." Essie lifts her chin defiantly.

"And let Papa starve?" In Cari's sweet, young voice, this does not sound okay, even to Essie.

"No one is going to starve," Tía Lola repeats. *"Se lo prometo!"*

"I promise, too." Juanita raises her right hand. "Me, Tía Lola, and Miguel do solemnly pledge that we will never ever let the Swords starve." Juanita is hoping to inject some humor into the grim gathering, but nobody laughs. "I'll bring you food from our house," she adds, more to the point.

"Especially all her vegetables," Miguel jokes.

Juanita scowls at her brother. Miguel has been in sixth grade only a week, and he's already such a know-it-all.

"Okay, people, let's try really, really hard," Victoria says, stepping in again to avoid sparks. Now that her father is dating Miguel and Juanita's mother, Victoria is being kept busy putting out fires in *both* families. "I'm sure that we can figure out a way to earn tons of money."

Silence greets this hopeful pronouncement. Even Tía Lola is looking frustrated. The beauty mark above her right eye is lost in her wrinkled brow.

"There's *sooooo* much talent in this room!" Victoria is beginning to sound desperate, even to her own ears. Like a cheerleader for a team that has never won a game and never will.

Essie's face suddenly brightens. She is remembering the genuine samurai sword Colonel Charlebois gave her this past summer. "I could give sword-fighting lessons."

3

"Way to go, Essie!" Victoria says, trying to sound enthusiastic. But she doubts that sword-fighting lessons will be in big demand in a small town in Vermont. Still, it's important to encourage Essie those rare times when she is being positive. Victoria writes down "sword fighting?" on the SOS list on her clipboard.

"And baseball lessons," Essie continues, now positively on a roll. An awesome pitcher and a home-run hitter, Essie is always looking for someone to practice with—and a few of Miguel's teammates have taken her up on it. So maybe she should charge for her time. "You want to help me, Miguel?"

Miguel doesn't like the idea of charging his friends, but he can't come up with any other way to help. Given that Víctor, the Swords' father, might someday marry his mother, it's too bad that no one in their combined families has a lot of money. His own father, Papi, is an artist whose day job—decorating department store windows down in New York City—is not a big moneymaker. Papi's fiancée, Carmen, is a lawyer, but like Víctor, who worked in the same firm up till a month ago, Carmen does a lot of free work. So what the right hand earns, the left hand gives away.

The only rich person they all know is Colonel Charlebois, who has been super generous with both families. In fact, neither family would have a roof over its head if it weren't for him. It was Colonel Charlebois who rented his old farmhouse to Miguel and Juanita and Mami when they first moved to Vermont. Then, when the colonel learned Mami was looking for their very own house to

4

buy, he very generously turned the rent payments into house payments. The farmhouse on ten acres is on its way to becoming theirs.

Now the colonel has taken in the Espadas, though he claims it has nothing to do with helping them. Even before the Espadas decided to move to Vermont, the colonel had made up his mind to share his big house in town with housemates. He was too lonely living by himself, after spending his whole life surrounded by hundreds and thousands of soldiers in the army.

But so far, the colonel has refused any payment until Víctor has found a job, which he hasn't. It seems the last thing this small town needs is another lawyer.

This might turn out to be a blessing in disguise. A few nights ago, Víctor admitted to his daughters (and this is a family secret, so it'd be great if it were kept between the covers of this book) that for a long time now, he has not been happy practicing law. Too much arguing. Too many people in trouble.

But what could he do instead?

Papa isn't sure. Growing up poor, he had to work to help out his family and put himself through school. He used to dream of playing baseball, or at the very least, coaching it. But he has already contacted all the local schools, and everyone is set with their sports staff for the year. "I'll find something, don't worry," he has assured his daughters. "Maybe a job where I can make people happy for a change. And hey, guess what? I've already got the best job of all, being your father." Too bad that being a parent is not a paying job.

Victoria is looking around the room. "Any more ideas?" Five kids, an intelligent dog, a magical *tía,* surely they can come up with one moneymaking scheme!

Juanita has been wondering what she can do that someone might pay her for. Suddenly it occurs to her. "Remember how everyone this last summer loved my flowers and kept saying they wanted me to come over and help out in their garden?" Tía Lola nods energetically, which sort of makes up for the fact that no one else remembers this compliment. "I can sign up people to help them with their flowers!"

She is so excited that even her know-it-all brother doesn't have the heart to remind her that it is mid-September. Vermont is headed for winter. The Swords *will* starve if they have to wait for grocery money until gardening weather in April.

Victoria wishes she could offer babysitting, but Papa has refused even to discuss the idea until Victoria turns thirteen, which won't be until next February. And that's just *discussing* the idea, not *letting* her do it. Meanwhile, Papa is perfectly okay with letting Victoria babysit her sisters without paying her for it.

"I could cook and clean people's houses and take in sewing and ironing." Tía Lola is rattling off everything and anything she can think of to do. "And I could give Spanish lessons, cooking lessons, dance lessons—"

"Oh, oh, oh!" Cari is waving her hand. She has just started kindergarten, where raising your hand is such a big rule that now she raises her hand even at home. "I can give ballet lessons!" She is so proud of herself for thinking of something to keep her family from starving.

"You can't teach ballet! You're only five years old." Essie would have to be the naysayer.

But Cari is already on her toes doing a pirouette to prove she can so teach ballet. Everyone claps. "I can also teach handstands!" She tries one, but overdoes the swing of her legs and flops over on the floor. Who cares? It's the effort that counts. Everyone claps again.

Everyone but Essie, who rolls her eyes. But before she can naysay handstand lessons, Essie is stopped by a look from her older sister. It's one of those if-looks-could-kill looks that Victoria is so good at. Maybe her older sister should hire herself out as a hit man. No fingerprints, no smoking gun. Just a glance. She'd be in high demand. No one would suspect the sweet, responsible Victoria of being a killer.

But Victoria isn't feeling particularly sweet or responsible. She glances down at her list. Except for Tía Lola's offers, the rest are ridiculous! Baseball tutoring? Sword fighting? Handstand and ballet lessons given by a five-year-old? It takes all of Victoria's self-control not to bunch up her sheet of paper and toss it into the trash can.

❋❋❋

As they ride their bikes home from town, Tía Lola and Miguel and Juanita are quiet. Each one is still preoccupied with how to help the Espada family.

At the corner of their road stands the two-story house where Papi and Carmen have sometimes stayed on week-

7

end visits. Tía Lola stops, head cocked, reading the sign:
BRIDGEPORT B&B

"Miguel and Juanita, I always forget to ask when we pass this place. Why don't the owners finish the sign?"

"Finish it, Tía Lola?" Miguel doesn't understand. It's the same old, weathered sign that's been up since before they moved to this road.

"Aren't the owners going to spell out their names?"

Miguel smiles, amused. Tía Lola arrived in the United States only last year, and sometimes she doesn't understand how things work here. "A B&B is the name of a kind of hotel in someone's house, like staying with a friend, but you have to pay for it."

"That's a shame," Tía Lola says, shaking her head in disapproval. "To charge your friends."

"But they're not really your friends," Juanita adds. "It's just a way for a family to earn some money. Using their own house as a hotel."

A look has come over Tía Lola's face that Miguel and Juanita know well. The opposite of a if-looks-could-kill look; it is a if-looks-could-save-the-world look. The beauty mark on her forehead glows like a bright star. Some fun and fantastic idea is brewing in their aunt's head. Before they can stop her, Tía Lola has turned her bicycle around and is pedaling back to town. "Hey, Tía Lola! It's this way to our house!"

But Tía Lola can't hear them. By now she is a distant blur. And all Juanita and Miguel can do is turn their bikes around and try to catch up with her.

8

"I have a solution!" Tía Lola has burst into the room where Colonel Charlebois and the Espada girls have just sat down to tea. Miguel and Juanita trail in behind her. All three are out of breath after their fast and furious bike ride into town.

"What on earth are you talking about?" Colonel Charlebois exclaims once he has settled Tía Lola in a chair. "A solution to what?"

"Oh, just a family project," Victoria says vaguely. She casts a warning look over at Essie and Juanita, the two blabbermouths. If they confess to the colonel that Papa doesn't want to be a lawyer anymore and can't find any other job, the colonel is liable to throw the Espadas out of the house. No, wait; that's not what the kind old man would do. He'd probably try to give them charity, which Papa would never accept. Victoria doesn't get why her father has to be so against charity. After all, he named his own baby girl Caridad, which means "charity" in Spanish.

The colonel rises from his chair. "If you'd like to have this conversation in private . . ."

"No, *coronel, por favor,* you must stay." Tía Lola has finally caught her breath. Her heart has settled down. "This solution will require your permission and participation."

Now it's the colonel's heart doing a little skip and jump. Not since his army days traveling all over the world has he felt this stirring of excitement. There's life in the old man yet! He sits back down in his chair, eyes gleaming. "Go on."

First things first. "What does a B&B stand for?" Tía Lola asks.

9

"A bed-and-breakfast," the colonel says without hesitation. "Guests pay for a bed and their breakfast."

"And how much does this guest pay for this bed and this breakfast?"

"Oh, I don't know. I'm not in the market for a B&B, so I've not kept up with prices. Why are you asking, if I may ask?"

"*Bueno, coronel,* you may soon be in the market for a B&B, so if you would be so kind as to find out what it costs, we—"

"You mean you're throwing me out of my own house?" the colonel cuts her off gruffly. He has a look of alarm on his face, but there is a twinkle in his eye.

"*Ay, coronel,* where are my manners?" Tía Lola has forgotten to ask first if the colonel would entertain her moneymaking solution. "Remember how you said you prefer living with company?"

"Well, yes. But I've got very fine company here now." He nods at the three Espada girls, who are all looking quite perplexed.

"But they are your renters, and I am speaking of guests."

"Guests, you say?" The colonel scowls, but even the Espada girls, who have known him only a couple of months, can tell he is intrigued. "But where will we put them?"

"Here is my proposal."

They all pull their chairs around the tea table as Tía Lola draws a ground plan of Colonel Charlebois's house. On the first floor, the colonel can keep his bedroom. But if the Espadas move one floor up to the little attic rooms, that would free up three bedrooms on the second floor for B&B guests. "What do you think, *coronel*?"

Everyone turns expectantly to the old man. The Espada girls are ready to throw themselves at his feet and beg him to please, please, please let them run a B&B out of his house.

This could be sooooo exciting, Victoria is thinking. Maybe a family with teenage boys will stay here. Papa has absolutely ruled out even talking about dating until Victoria is in high school. But if boys are guests, Victoria can hang out with them and not have to disobey her father.

Maybe a famous baseball player will come to their B&B and befriend the amazing athlete Esperanza Espada. Essie's heart soars. She can already see herself at Fenway Park, a guest of the Red Sox, sitting in their dugout.

Cari doesn't care who comes, just as long as it's not someone scary. But then she remembers Colonel Charlebois is a hero with medals for his bravery. He would defend her. And there's always Valentino.

Although this B&B won't be in their house, Miguel and Juanita are excited, too. First of all, anything Tía Lola thinks up is sure to be fun. Second, winter is coming, that boring time of year when you can't go outside and play baseball or grow flowers. It'll be good to have a fun project in town.

Colonel Charlebois takes a big breath, as if he were about to blow out all eighty-five candles that will be on his birthday cake this December. "I think it's a terrific idea!"

A cheer goes up. High-fiving all around.

"What shall we call our B&B?" The colonel looks around the room.

"I know, I know!" Cari raises her hand, but she doesn't wait to be called on. "Let's call it Tía Lola's B&B." She puffs out her little chest with pride at being the first to come up with the best name in the world.

Tía Lola thanks Cari, but she cannot accept this great honor. "It is Colonel Charlebois's house. It must be 'Colonel Charlebois's B&B.'"

But the colonel disagrees. "Sounds too much like a military barracks. No one will want to stay here. Don't you see, Tía Lola? Your name adds a touch of exoticism—"

"What's exorcism?" Cari wants to know. After all, the name was her idea, so she wants to understand what kind of touch her suggestion is adding.

"Ex-o-ti-cism," Colonel Charlebois pronounces. "It means something out of the ordinary, exciting, and enchanting." The children's faces light up, but Tía Lola keeps shaking her head.

Victoria steps in. "We'll settle it with a vote. How many for 'Tía Lola's B&B'?"

Everyone except Tía Lola raises their hand. Valentino barks his agreement.

"'Tía Lola's B&B,' it'll be!" Victoria announces. Everyone except Tía Lola is on their feet cheering.

Cari suddenly remembers. "Doesn't Papa have to vote, too?"

It's as if someone has thrown a big bucket of icy water on their fired-up heads and hearts. They all let themselves slowly back down into their chairs.

"I guess Papa does have to vote." Victoria is nothing if not fair.

"Well, that's the end of that solution," Essie says in a gloomy voice. "You know Papa, and how he doesn't want to impose on Colonel Charlebois."

"This is my house!" Colonel Charlebois reminds her. "I can do what I want here."

"Try telling that to Papa." Victoria sighs. Valentino, who understands the language of sighs, comes over and licks her hand.

It's as if a glove has been flung in challenge at the old soldier. "I *will* tell him. If I want to turn my house into Tía Lola's B&B, you better believe I will, no matter what Víctor Espada has to say about it!"

They're all back on their feet again, high-fiving and cheering. Which is why no one hears the front door open or the footsteps coming down the hall toward the room where there's quite a commotion going on.

Papa is at the door, arms folded, looking disapprovingly at his daughters. "Girls, you need to keep your voices down. This is Colonel Charlebois's house." For some reason, his reminder brings on a renewed round of loud laughter.

"Would someone care to tell me what is going on?" Papa asks sternly.

The children all raise their hands.

But Colonel Charlebois pulls rank. "I'll do the explaining here," he says. "After all, this *is* my house."

13

chapter two

How the Parents Came Around and Around
and Around

Papa's first response to the idea of a B&B in Colonel Charlebois's house is no surprise. "Absolutely not!"

"But, Víctor, you say yourself you are unhappy practicing law because people are always arguing," Tía Lola reminds him. "What you love is making people happy."

"Where did you get that idea?" Víctor asks. The question is addressed to Tía Lola, but Papa is looking pointedly at his three daughters as if he already knows the answer.

"I'm sorry, Papa." Victoria knows her father's change of heart is a family secret. But Miguel and Juanita are like a brother and sister, and Tía Lola is like a special aunt and second mother rolled into one.

Papa can't deny being pleased that his daughters have formed such a strong bond with Linda's children and aunt.

14

But what good will that do him if Linda breaks up with him? And who could blame her for getting cold feet at the prospect of marrying an unemployed man with three young daughters?

"This will be an opportunity to make people happy, to make yourself happy." Tía Lola goes on to describe the many guests who will come to their B&B, the happy times they will have, the oodles of money these guests will spend. "They will shop at Estargazer's store; they will eat at Rudy's café; they will get gas at Johnny's Garage and buy pet supplies at Petey's shop. You will be helping us all by agreeing to this plan, Víctor."

Initially, Víctor dismissed the idea because he feared imposing on the colonel. But now it seems that by agreeing to a B&B, Víctor will actually be saving the small town of Bridgeport from bankruptcy.

This is how Víctor comes around.

● ● ●

But by the next evening, Víctor has changed his mind.

"Sorry, guys," he tells the group around the table. He and his daughters are having dinner with Linda's family at the farmhouse. "But it really is too much of an imposition on Colonel Charlebois. We have to remember the colonel is not a young man. How old did you say he was going to be?" he adds, glancing over at Linda.

But before Mami can answer, Essie has raised an outcry. "Papa, you heard him yourself, Colonel Charlebois *wants* to do a B&B!" Essie is close to tears, which is not like Essie at all. "He really did," she assures Linda. "Right?" Tía Lola and the kids all nod.

15

Linda is looking torn. She doesn't want to disappoint any of the children, especially Víctor's daughters, whose mother died three years ago. Víctor has been raising them on his own. Mami herself lost both her parents when she was a little girl, even younger than Cari. She was so lucky that Tía Lola stepped in to raise her. These girls need that same kind of lucky break. "A hotel takes a lot of work," she tries to reason with them. "You're all going to be super busy with school. And Tía Lola is teaching Spanish this year."

"I only teach twice a week," Tía Lola points out. "Our B&B will open just on weekends." They decided this back at Colonel Charlebois's house. Start slow. See how it goes.

"We want to start slow, see how it goes," Victoria says, ever the peacemaker. "And Papa isn't working. In fact, the whole reason . . ." Victoria catches herself, as her father is beaming a big red stop sign at her.

Thankfully, Linda doesn't seem to notice. "Remember, your father will soon have his hands full with cases and clients."

This is the moment when Papa should confess that he doesn't want to practice law anymore. Instead, he casts an apologetic glance over at his brood and runs his hand through his black hair, which is what he does when he is feeling confused as to what to say or do.

❋❋❋

"I just don't get why Papa won't tell her the truth." Essie looks over at Miguel and Juanita, as if they should know the answer just because Mami is their mother.

The children have gathered up in Tía Lola's room after

16

supper to discuss the situation before the Swords head back to town.

"Víctor is probably afraid of disappointing Linda," Tía Lola explains.

"But Mami would understand." Juanita is sure of it. After all, her mother is a psychologist. People confess stuff to her all the time.

"I think you're right, Juanita," Tía Lola agrees. "But Víctor knows how hard a time your *mami* had when she was married to your *papi*. There was never enough money." The way Tía Lola explains it, Juanita and Miguel don't feel like their aunt is blaming either parent. Just explaining why their mother might not want to marry a man who isn't earning any money.

"But if Víctor runs a B&B, he will be earning money!" Juanita throws her two hands in the air. How can Mami not understand something so simple? Juanita is only in fourth grade, but sometimes she feels a lot smarter than her own mother.

Suddenly—or are they imagining it?—the room is growing brighter! But the light is not coming from Tía Lola's bedside lamp, but from the brilliant idea inside her head.

"The thin edge of the wedge," Tía Lola says mysteriously.

"The what of the what? It sounds like a sandwich, Tía Lola." Juanita giggles.

Tía Lola explains. "You know how sometimes we can't open a jammed door? So what do we do? We squeeze the thin edge of a wedge into the crack and pry the door open."

Five young faces are looking expectantly at Tía Lola, waiting for the great illumination to come to them. What on earth does an unstuck door have to do with their B&B and convincing Mami and Papa?

"The B&B idea is stuck, *no es verdad*?" Isn't this so? Yes, they would all have to agree that this is so. "It's too big and scary an idea for Mami to agree to." Now Cari is really nodding. She understands about scary things. "And Víctor is stuck, too, as he isn't ready to confess he doesn't want to be a lawyer anymore. But what if we were to suggest just starting with a guinea-pig weekend?"

"But we don't know any guinea pigs who want to go to a B&B," Juanita says, being silly.

"Valentino can pretend to be a guinea pig, right, Valentino?" Cari volunteers him. Valentino, always a good sport, half raises himself from Tía Lola's flowered rug. Of course he'll help out any way he can.

But Tía Lola says they need human guinea pigs. Some guests to stay at the house—for free, since this is a trial run—to prove to Mami that it can be done with minimum hassle to Colonel Charlebois and the Espada family. Meanwhile, once Papa gets a taste of running a place where he can make people happy, he's going to feel confident enough to confess to Mami.

"Tía Lola"—Essie is shaking her head—"you are absolutely *the* most incredible genius I have ever known." Excepting Essie herself, of course. But it would be immodest for her to say so.

They troop downstairs to present the thin edge of the wedge to Víctor and Linda. And how can Mami and Papa resist the determination, the reasoned arguments, the barking pleas, the excitement and enthusiasm of the assembled group of five children, one aunt, and a dog ready to turn himself into a guinea pig to convince them to give the idea a try? They all go down on bended knees, even Valentino, which is not so easy for a four-legged animal.

Mami is having a hard time trying not to smile. "Just one weekend," she agrees tentatively. One weekend is nothing, a mere two days. The kids will get it out of their system, and Víctor and Colonel Charlebois will be rid of this B&B lunacy. "So who will you recruit for your first guests?"

They have all been so intent on convincing Mami and Papa that they never discussed who to invite to be their guinea pigs.

This time it's Miguel who comes up with the solution. Papi and Carmen are driving up next weekend to celebrate Juanita's birthday. Instead of staying at the B&B down the road, they can stay at Tía Lola's B&B instead.

"Well . . ." Mami looks over at Víctor. "If it's okay with you?"

Miguel can almost hear the creaking of a door being slowly wedged open.

●●●

Now that two parents have come around (and around), it's time to ask the third parent to join them.

Since it was his idea, Miguel calls up Papi. "We want you to be our gue—guests at Tía Lola's B&B this weekend."

"Wait a minute, *mi'jo*." Papi stops Miguel. *"Mi'jo,"* "my

19

son," is Papi's affectionate term for Miguel. Sometimes when his father calls him that, it makes Miguel wistful, thinking of how it used to be living with Papi under the same roof. "Let me get this straight, your mother and Tía Lola are turning the house into a B&B? What about her job at the college? And isn't Tía Lola still teaching Spanish at the school?"

"No, Papi, listen. Tía Lola's B&B is actually over at Colonel Charlebois's house. And it's just on weekends."

"I see," Papi says, but Miguel can tell that Papi is still confused. "How about Abuelito and Abuelita? They want to come, too, for Juanita's birthday."

"There's plenty of room at Tía Lola's B&B." Miguel is sure of it. Three whole bedrooms on the second floor, to be exact. In fact, there's even room for Juanita and Miguel and Tía Lola up in the attic. "We're staying over to help run it."

"We were just going to ask your *mami* if we could crash at the farmhouse again. No offense, but that B&B down the road . . ." Papi hasn't wanted to complain, but the owner is not a very pleasant person.

"But this'll be so awesome, Papi. We can all be together right in town." Except, of course, for Mami. But Miguel gets to live with his mother year-round.

"I guess." Papi pauses, considering. In the silence, Miguel hears another door being pried open. "If you really think Víctor and your *mami* are cool with it, sure. Tía Lola's B&B it'll be. So, oink oink. We'll be your guinea pigs."

Miguel can't help laughing. Papi doesn't mind being a

guinea pig one bit. It reminds Miguel of the old days, when Papi lived with them. His father could always make him laugh. "Love you, Papi," Miguel blurts out, a phrase he's usually too embarrassed to say—even to his parents—now that he's in the sixth grade.

●●●

Tía Lola and all the kids set to work preparing the second floor to be a B&B. "A *temporary* B&B," they add when Papa or Mami is within earshot.

"That's a lot of trouble for temporary," Papa remarks. Since he and Linda agreed to a trial weekend, there has been a tremendous amount of scurrying around and rearranging furniture and moving belongings upstairs to the attic rooms of the colonel's house.

"We have to really turn it into a B&B for the weekend, or how can we know what it's like to run one?" Sometimes Essie has to explain the simplest things to her father. Just like Juanita with her mother.

"And just think, Papa, it'll be a way to make our rooms even nicer, if we move back down," Victoria points out. This argument is sure to convince her father, who has gotten very strict about keeping their rooms tidy since they moved in with Colonel Charlebois.

Cari is having the best time of all. It's like playing house with a real house and with everyone participating. Usually Cari can't get anyone to play what Essie calls her "baby games" with her. Except Valentino.

Víctor shakes his head at his daughters' combined persuasive powers. They should all three be lawyers! But he joins in the effort of setting up Tía Lola's B&B with more gusto than he expected of himself. This *is* fun, he keeps thinking.

Colonel Charlebois is having fun, too, enjoying all the life that has flooded back into his house. But Mami still worries that all this upheaval is an imposition on the kindly old man. In order to spare him the commotion of a guinea-pig B&B, she invites him to stay with her this weekend. She'll be all alone, as the kids and Tía Lola will be sleeping over as part of the staff at the B&B. Although the colonel has been looking forward to the excitement, he cannot resist the chance to stay at his childhood home for two days.

The Swords are soon relocated to the attic, where each one has a tiny room. Now it's time to tackle the three vacant-looking bedrooms on the second floor.

"I think we should have themes," Essie suggests. "You know, a baseball theme in one room, a tropical theme in another."

"I can really help with that one," Juanita offers. After all, she and Tía Lola turned her own bedroom into a tropical paradise. Her four-poster is painted to look like palm trees, with fronds forming a canopy above her mattress. A parrot piñata hangs from the ceiling. Just being in her room is like going on a Caribbean vacation.

"I have extra posters and stuff," Miguel offers for the baseball room.

"Maybe your father can paint a field of dreams on the walls, you think?" Essie recalls the beautiful painting Miguel's father did of a baseball field. It was quite the sensation when Papi unrolled it at the first big game that Miguel's team played this past summer.

"Now, hold on there, Essie." Her father has come around to liking this B&B idea. However, painting the colonel's walls with murals is out of the question.

But Colonel Charlebois is all for Essie's "brilliant suggestions." They are two peas in a pod, always delighted by the crazy ideas the other one comes up with.

"We've got the baseball theme and the tropical theme. What about the third bedroom?" Victoria asks. She's got that clipboard out again and is making lists of what sorts of things will be needed for each room.

"Well, this is New England; we should consider a colonial theme," Papa proposes. They could go over to Fort Ticonderoga and visit the gift shop. "They have some authentic memorabilia." Oh no, Papa is about to ruin everything, the big history buff. He'll soon turn the room into a museum with a velvet cord across the doorway.

"I really think we should have one room that's kind of . . . you know . . . sort of . . ." Victoria knows if she says "romantic," Essie will stick her forefinger in her open mouth and pretend to be gagging. Papa has told her that it's an offensive way to show disagreement. But that's never stopped Essie from being a repeat offender. "I mean, what if a newlywed couple want to come for their honeymoon?"

"They'd come to our B&B?" Papa is doubtful.

"I would," Victoria says brightly. "Not that I'm getting married any time soon," she adds, because Papa is looking at her with *that* look, like she'd better be careful, or he's going to padlock her in one of these rooms until she's at least twenty-one.

By Friday afternoon, Tía Lola's B&B is ready to receive its first guests. The lush, colorful tropical room is reserved for Abuelito and Abuelita, who will feel like they're back home on the island. Tía Carmen, as the Sword girls affectionately call their father's former colleague, will absolutely adore the bridal bedroom, especially with her own wedding to Papi coming up sometime soon. (They have not yet fixed a date.) Meanwhile, Papi is going to love his baseball room. Although he does not play the sport, he is a huge Yankees fan. But the best part of his room will be the inflatable mattress beside the bed, where his son, *mi'jo,* will sleep, both under the same roof just like the old days.

chapter three

How the Guinea-Pig Weekend Almost Met
with Total Disaster

It is Friday night of the guinea-pig weekend at Tía Lola's B&B. The guests are being shown to their rooms before walking down the block to dinner at Rudy's café.

Since its theme was her idea, Victoria gets to escort Carmen to the romantic bedroom.

"It's like a bride's fantasy in here!" Carmen exclaims, turning circles in delight. The curtains are lacy and white and held back by pale pink sashes. The bed is strewn with rose petals, and there's a white canopy overhead with little doves dangling down. Even the air smells perfumed with roses.

"Do you really like it?" Victoria asks timidly.

"What do you mean? I adore it!" Carmen cries, hugging the pleased girl.

25

Victoria is relieved. Most of the little touches were her idea. But for days, every time Essie would walk by the room, she'd pretend she was going to be sick.

Next door, Abuelita and Abuelito are full of admiration for their tropical bedroom. *"¡Un paradiso de verdad!"* they tell Cari and Juanita. A real paradise. "Like being back in the Dominican Republic!" Who would have thought that by driving six hours north, Abuelito and Abuelita would feel closer to the tropical island they miss so much?

Meanwhile, at the end of the hall, Víctor and Essie and Miguel are showing Papi his room. It is packed with baseball memorabilia, including a life-size cutout of David Ortiz standing guard by the door. Even though Miguel's *papi* is a Yankees fan, he loves the Red Sox slugger Big Papi, whose name he shares. "Amazing how you guys pulled this together." Papi shakes his head in disbelief. Suddenly his eye is caught by the sign above the bed. "Is this for real? I mean, I thought we were your first guests."

"You *are* our first guests," Víctor confirms.

"But what about that sign?"

Víctor looks in the direction Papi is pointing. "Essie?" Víctor asks like it's a question, but he already seems to know the answer.

"Well, it's just decoration . . . ," Essie grumbles.

"It's false advertising, is what it is." Even if he doesn't practice law ever again, Papa will never get rid of the lawyer he once was. "Please remove it, Essie."

But Miguel's father persuades Víctor to keep the sign with a slight revision. Using Essie's marker, Papi inserts a few teensy words, so that the sign now accurately reads:

26

I wish ⌃ had ⌃
DAVID ORTIZ SLEPT HERE

Meanwhile, upstairs in the attic, Tía Lola has finished unpacking her things in the big front attic room, where she will be sleeping. It's a large, cozy room, where the kids like to hold their meetings. A bank of windows looks out on the street, so Tía Lola can check on the comings and goings of her guests. She also has a bird's-eye view of the majestic maple tree with brilliant leaves in the front yard. Tía Lola opens the window and leans out to take a breath of fresh air.

Suddenly she remembers the letter. She sits down on the foldout couch and pulls the envelope out of her pocket.

●●●

This morning, Tía Lola had set out to town on her bicycle to put the finishing touches on Colonel Charlebois's house while the children were all in school and Mami was at work. As Tía Lola was riding past the house with the B&B sign, a big, red-faced woman rushed out and flagged her down.

"*Buenos días,* good morning! How are you?" Tía Lola began. Not that she needed to ask. She could already tell from the look on the B&B woman's face, and the violent way she thrust the letter at Tía Lola's chest, like a punch, that the lady was very angry.

"*¿Qué pasa?*" Tía Lola blurted out. What was wrong? By now, she knew enough English to be able to ask this

27

question in her new language. But she was so flabbergasted by the punched missive that the words tumbled out of her mouth in Spanish.

"This is America, and in case you haven't noticed, we speak ENGLISH in this country." The way the lady said "ENGLISH" made spit spray from her mouth.

Tía Lola wiped her face with her lucky yellow scarf, which made her feel better. "I can speak a little English, Mrs. B&B," she offered in a friendly voice.

"My name is not Mrs. B&B!" the lady snapped back. "I'm Odette Beauregard. *Mrs.* Beauregard to you."

"Very pleased to make your acquaintance, Mrs. Beauregard." Tía Lola was about to give the woman a kiss on the cheek, which is how Tía Lola normally greets everybody. But Tía Lola was left kissing the air. The woman had already turned on her heels and marched back into her house, slamming the door behind her, although there was a sign on it saying DO NOT LET THE DOOR SLAM.

Tía Lola stood gazing at the unpainted, ramshackle house with the VACANCY sign out front. What could have upset the woman so? As she was getting back on her bike, Tía Lola caught sight of a pale girl who had been raking leaves in the backyard. She lifted a hand in greeting. Tía Lola waved back, but she didn't dare say a word, as the poor girl looked terrified.

Tía Lola stuck the letter in her pocket and rode into town. She didn't actually forget the incident, but soon she was caught up in all there was to do: checking all the guest rooms; making her little animal candies; drawing up the breakfast menus and going grocery shopping with Víctor.

28

Then the kids all came back from school. Mami swung by after work to pick up the colonel and his suitcase. The guinea-pig guests arrived shortly thereafter and had to be settled in. At long last, everybody is taking a short rest before setting out for the dinner special that Rudy is offering at his café to all of Tía Lola's guests.

Tía Lola gazes down at the envelope in her hand. It is addressed, "To Tía Lola's B&B." How did the woman even know that Tía Lola's B&B was in the works? There is no sign up front. There has been no notice in the paper. In fact, only two people in town know of the B&B plan: Rudy, of course, as they had to tell him in order to arrange the dinner special for their guests; and Stargazer, who helped out with some of the decorating, including ordering things like the dangling doves, the Big Papi cutout, the parrot lamp that sits on the bedside table between the two beds in Abuelito and Abuelita's room.

So how did Mrs. Beauregard find out about Tía Lola's B&B? Only one way that Tía Lola can figure out. Her little niece Juanita finds it extremely hard to keep a secret. Just yesterday, Juanita mentioned the visit she had with Mrs. Beauregard's daughter, who actually bought three boxes of the chocolate mints Juanita was selling to help pay for her class's field trips this year. The teenage daughter was in the backyard raking leaves and waved her over. She seemed so lonely. What was really weird is that she asked Juanita not to mention the purchase to her mother, if Juanita happened to run into her.

Juanita would not want to hurt the daughter's feelings, but if she ever saw Mrs. Beauregard coming toward her, sorry, but Juanita would run *away* from her. In fact, the only reason Juanita even stepped foot on the property was because she'd already seen Mrs. Beauregard pulling out of her driveway in her big black Buick.

Tía Lola opens the envelope and unfolds the letter. Of course, it is written in English, but Tía Lola can tell that Mrs. Beauregard is very upset: the handwriting looks like slashes on the page. Something something about "a foreigner opening a B&B." Then something something about "decent Americans being prevented from earning a living because of people like you." On and on and on. Toward the end of the letter, Tía Lola can pick out the words "report" and "authorities." Mrs. Beauregard is threatening to report Tía Lola to the authorities? But what has Tía Lola done wrong that she should get in trouble for?

Tía Lola considers taking the letter to the children or to Víctor to translate. But why ruin this guinea-pig weekend with unpleasant news? A nice dinner awaits them at Amigos Café, and then tomorrow, Juanita's birthday. Mami and Tía Lola have planned a party out at the farmhouse. All week, Víctor and the colonel and the children have been so happy. Tía Lola folds the letter back in the envelope and puts the envelope in her pocket.

●●●

Dinner at Amigos Café is not only delicious, but homey, like a meal at a friend's house, including as many helpings as you want at no extra charge.

Everyone lingers over dessert, even Abuelito and Abuelita, who are usually in bed by now.

As the talk starts winding down, Tía Lola slips out of

30

the restaurant and walks down the street to the colonel's house. She wants to be sure to turn on the outdoor lights so her guests don't trip on the cracks in the sidewalk or crash into the prickly holly bush on their way back. She'll also pull down the shades in each bedroom and fold back the blankets, just like in fancy hotels. On each pillow, she will place a little surprise: a candied guinea pig she made earlier today—an inside joke the children will appreciate.

To Tía Lola's astonishment, the front door and—when she checks—the back door are locked! All the windows are secure. What is going on? Tía Lola is sure she left the front door unlocked, as they were just going down the block to Amigos Café. Nobody in Bridgeport ever locks up their house, unless they are going to be away for a long time, like the snowbirds who head for Florida before the first snowfall.

In just a few minutes, Tía Lola's B&B guests are going to be coming down the sidewalk, exhausted after a long drive and a big dinner. The last thing they need is to be locked out of their B&B and have to find alternative accommodations until a locksmith can come in the morning. What to do?

After trying a few windows again, without luck, Tía Lola recalls one window that she is sure is open. The only problem is that it is three stories up in her attic bedroom! Just as she's wondering what to do, Tía Lola hears the rustling of leaves as the wind blows through the maple tree. Tía Lola speaks Spanish and a little English, but until this moment, she had no idea she could understand trees.

Tía Lola, climb me! the maple is saying.

Tía Lola gazes up and up at the tall tree. It has been a good forty-five years since she was a girl and climbed any kind of a tree. *Con paciencia y con calma, se subió un burro en una palma,* she reminds herself, a favorite saying of hers. With patience and calm, even a burro can climb a palm tree.

Tía Lola isn't sure that she can climb a maple tree, no matter how calm or patient she is. But she must try. Mami will no doubt view any fiasco as proof that this B&B is a foolish idea. Tía Lola must save this guinea-pig weekend from disaster! She lifts the hem of her flowered skirt and tucks it into her waistband. Then for good luck, she kisses the yellow scarf tied around her neck.

"One, two, three!" she whispers. But Tía Lola is still standing on the ground at the count of three, looking up at the tall tree. Maybe she needs to count in Spanish instead? *"¡Uno, dos, tres!"* she starts over. At the count of *tres,* Tía Lola is still standing in front of Colonel Charlebois's house, her two feet firmly on the ground.

But that lucky scarf works wonders. It just so happens that when Tía Lola stepped out of Amigos Café, one person noticed her departure. This person happens to be a pro at climbing trees. In fact, if there were a tree-climbing category in the Olympics, this person would stand a good chance of winning the gold.

As Miguel hurries down the street after his aunt, a car turns the corner and lights up a figure in front of Colonel Charlebois's house. Tía Lola! She looks like she just took a flying leap off the ground and caught hold of a low branch on the maple tree. Now she is dangling there with a surprised look on her face. "Tía Lola," Miguel calls out. "What on earth are you doing?"

"I'm not *on* earth," Tía Lola calls back. That's the problem. She's three feet above the ground, holding on for dear life, too dizzy to look down and too frightened to climb up on the next branch.

Miguel runs over to where his aunt is hanging like a Christmas ornament. A terrified Christmas ornament. "Get down, Tía Lola," Miguel calls up to his aunt.

"But I don't want to get down. I want to get up!" Tía Lola explains. And then, very briefly, since it's hard to go into details when you are hanging from a tree and slowly losing your grip, Tía Lola tells her nephew the problem. The house is locked. They have to get inside to turn on the lights so their guests can find their way safely back. The only open window is the one in her attic bedroom, which looks out onto the maple tree.

"I'll get it, Tía Lola. You just get down, okay?"

Before Tía Lola has landed on the ground, Miguel is halfway up the maple tree. Soon Tía Lola can hear him scrambling through the window. Her attic-room light comes on. Seconds later, the hallway on the second floor lights up, then the first-floor entry light. The front door opens and her nephew is running out to check on her.

"Come on in, Tía Lola," Miguel says, helping his aunt to her feet.

As she stands up, Tía Lola wipes her sweaty brow with her yellow scarf. Off comes the beauty mark on her forehead, along with her perspiration. "Thank you so much, Miguel. You have saved the situation."

"No problem, Tía Lola. But I'm just curious. Why'd you lock the house? Are you afraid there's more burglars in town or something?" It doesn't seem like Tía Lola to expect the worst of anybody.

But right now Tía Lola is thinking the worst of a certain person who may very well want her new B&B to fail. But again, Tía Lola does not want to upset her nephew or ruin this weekend for anybody. And in the scheme of things, this really is a harmless prank. What else can go wrong, anyway?

Besides, now's not the time to try to solve the B&B lockdown mystery. They'd better hurry inside and get the bedrooms ready. Just this moment, a group of happy people are coming down the street toward the house. Leading the way is Colonel Charlebois, arm in arm with Mami and Víctor. Abuelita and Abuelito follow, hand in hand. The girls and Tía Carmen and Papi bring up the rear.

They are all tired, but their hearts are warm and their bellies are full. Up ahead is the lovely Victorian house where some of them will be sleeping. Beside it stands a majestic maple, like the ones in posters advertising New England vacations. The front walk is nicely lit, and inside, their sparkling rooms await them with beds turned down, shades pulled, and an adorable Vermont critter propped on each pillow, wishing them sweet dreams and a restful night.

Ahead stretch two happy days of fun and friendship, a dazzling success of a guinea-pig weekend. In fact, every guest will leave a tip on their bedside table and a little smiley face or thank-you or *gracias* penned on their guest notepads. And in the suggestion box, which an insecure Victoria and her worrywart father set up by the front door, they will find raves about how Tía Lola's B&B *has to* continue! Only two people know how close they came to disaster, and of those two, only one suspects who might be responsible.

chapter four

How Juanita Ran Away ~~from~~ Home

Juanita is feeling glum. Don't get her wrong, her birthday party was a blast. But now she has to wait a whole year before having another one.

From being *the* birthday girl, Juanita is back to being just another girl in a crowd. Even though her mother and Víctor aren't married, the two families are constantly together. Miguel still gets to be the only boy, but Juanita is now one of four girls. She's not spunky like Essie, or cute like Cari, or responsible like Victoria, so nobody notices Juanita-what's-her-name. In fact, Víctor can't seem to keep her straight: "Victoria, oops, Cari, I mean Essie, so sorry, Juanita."

Only with Papi does Juanita still get to be the one and only daughter. That, too, might change when Papi and Carmen get married. What if they have a baby? What if it's a boy? From all reports, little brothers are a pain in the butt. But what if it's a girl: a cute, spunky, responsible little sister who hogs all the attention away from Juanita?

Juanita wishes she could go back to being a little kid herself! Really little, like when she lived in New York City, and her parents were together, and she was in preschool with her best friend, Ming, who actually called yesterday in the middle of Juanita's birthday party. Juanita couldn't talk then, but she promised to call her friend back.

Sunday afternoon, after Papi and Carmen and her grandparents leave, Juanita asks Mami if she can call Ming.

"Have you finished your homework?"

"Not yet."

"You're a big girl now, Nita, honey. I shouldn't have to be reminding you to do your homework." Mami sighs, as if Juanita's being ten is tiring her out already.

As Juanita heads upstairs to tackle her homework, Mami has another reminder. "Don't forget to fold your clothes neatly in your drawers when you unpack your weekend bag. I shouldn't have to be picking up after you."

Had Juanita known that being ten would come with this laundry list of responsibilities, she would have given up having a birthday altogether.

"Remember, lights out promptly tonight. Now that you're a big girl, you're going to have to be a little better about getting yourself out to the bus on time."

The hard work of being a double-digit tween has begun.

Just as Juanita is finishing her homework, the phone rings. She's already halfway down the stairs when she hears her mother saying, "Let me see if she's available." It's as if Juanita is the president of a company who needs a secretary to schedule her phone conversations.

Mami has walked the phone out of the kitchen, covering the mouthpiece. "It's Ming," she says, and then unbelievably mouths, "Are you done with your homework?"

"Wow, that's horrible!" Ming commiserates when Juanita catches her up on what's been happening since she turned ten. "It sounds like a prison up there." Ming is nothing if not sympathetic. But sometimes her friend's sympathy makes Juanita feel even worse. "If my parents treated me like that, I'd—I don't know—I'd run away from home."

That is a great idea! Juanita will run away from home. That'll make Mami realize she can't be so hard on a new ten-year-old. "But where can I go?"

"You can come to our apartment. I'll hide you in my room. I'll bring you food from the table. When my parents go to work, you can come out and meet me at school."

As improbable as the plan sounds at first, it starts seeming possible the more Ming talks. All together, Juanita got just over a hundred dollars in cash for her birthday. That should cover a one-way bus ticket to New York City. Of course, once Juanita is on that bus, roaring away down the highways of her imagination, the plan becomes a little fuzzier and worrisome. How will Juanita get from the bus station to Ming's apartment? How will Ming let her in without her parents knowing?

After she hangs up, and Ming is no longer cheering

her on, Juanita begins to get cold feet. She can't help remembering how her brother got mugged last spring when they were visiting Papi, and Miguel took off on his own to Madison Square Garden.

That night, as Tía Lola is tucking her in, Juanita pours out her heart to her aunt. Tía Lola doesn't lecture Juanita about how, now that she is ten, she shouldn't entertain such juvenile ideas. In fact, Tía Lola totally understands. "I think everybody should run away at least once in their lives, preferably when they are young and have a lot of energy. Running away takes a lot of energy, you know?"

Juanita wouldn't know, but she nods.

"You can get very homesick, too." Tía Lola scrunches up her face, thinking really hard. "Hmmm. Let's see. How can we have the best parts of running away—the freedom, the adventures, the excitement—without the bad parts: the danger, the homesickness, no one to get our meals or tuck us in at night?"

Juanita is sure glad she confided in her aunt. Running away sounds a lot more complicated than Juanita first thought. "Maybe I can run away somewhere close by, so I can come home whenever I want. What do you think, Tía Lola?"

Tía Lola thinks this is a brilliant solution. "And I have just the place for you to run away to."

"You do?"

"Tía Lola's B&B!" Her aunt enumerates all the pluses of this plan: the B&B is empty during the week; Juanita already knows the colonel and the Swords, so she won't have to break important rules, like not talking to strangers;

meals will be provided; she won't have to miss school and end up flunking fourth grade.

Juanita already feels a lot better about this revised plan. But what about Ming? "She'll be so disappointed."

"I'm sure Ming is having second thoughts, too," Tía Lola guesses. "I think it's just that she misses you so much, she'll do anything to get to see you."

Juanita misses Ming, too, but she doesn't want to have to run away to New York to get to see her. It'd be so fun if Ming came here instead, and they ran away together to Tía Lola's B&B. But Ming's parents have never accepted Mami's invitation to visit. "It's like Vermont is mainland China," Mami has remarked to Juanita.

"So, what're we going to tell Mami?" As strict as her mother is being, Juanita would not want to worry her.

"You're thinking very responsibly, like an eleven- or twelve-year-old." Tía Lola is impressed. "Let's see. Most runaways leave a note behind. So you can write your *mami* and tell her where you'll be and how she can reach you. It's also a good idea to include when you might be back. Just so nobody moves into your room."

Juanita sits up, alarmed. "No one is moving in here!" Just because she is running away, she's not giving up her room.

"I know," Tía Lola agrees. "But that's why it's impor-tant to write a note." Her aunt pushes back the hair from her little niece's face and plants a kiss on her forehead. It occurs to Juanita that if she runs away, she won't be getting this special kiss every night.

"Can't you run away with me, Tía Lola?" Juanita

40

knows she sounds like a big baby, but running away won't be half as much fun if her aunt doesn't come along.

"Remember, I have to be here with your brother," Tía Lola reminds Juanita, whose face falls. "But after your *mami* gets home, I could ride my bike into town and spend the night with you. After all, you'll be the first runaway ever at my B&B. I wouldn't want you to get homesick and have to come right back."

No way! Juanita should be able to run away from home now that she is ten.

●●●

Juanita never realized that running away took so much planning. Which one of her stuffed animals will she bring along? Which favorite book? What outfits will she wear during her time away? And all of these supplies have to fit in her backpack along with her schoolbooks. The plan is for Juanita to get off the bus with Essie and Cari instead of riding it all the way out to their farmhouse after school.

Meanwhile, Mami seems to be improving. Along with emphasizing the responsibilities of being ten, Mami is also allowing Juanita some privileges: like letting her stay up a little later or watch certain movies with adult topics, like dating or murdering; or even permitting her to wear a lip gloss she got as a birthday present that has a little color in it.

But once you're caught up in an interesting plan, it's hard to abandon it. Besides, it'll be fun to stay at Tía Lola's B&B as a guest. It turns out that Juanita can have *any* guest room she wants. Then, on Friday, she will have to move upstairs with Essie. It's parents' weekend at the college, and all the rooms are filled.

Wednesday morning, Juanita leaves her runaway note taped to her bedroom door:

Dear Mami,

I am running away from home to Tía Lola's B&B. I love you very much, so PLEASE don't think that I am doing this because I want another mother. I just need some time to get used to being ten.

If Ming calls, please explain to her that I need to be a little older before I'm allowed to run away to New York City.

Okay, that's all, except for I should be done with running away by Friday, and then I'll stay to help with Tía Lola's B&B over the weekend, and then I'll come home.

xoxoxo,
Nita

P.S. Please don't let ANYBODY move into my room!!!

●●●

That afternoon, Juanita gets off the bus with Essie and Cari. "Hey, Nita!" Miguel calls out. "This isn't our stop."

"I'm running away," Juanita says breezily over her shoulder. It takes all her self-control not to turn around to watch the shock on her big brother's face.

Juanita follows the Swords into the house. Colonel

Charlebois is snoring away in the front parlor, Valentino asleep at his feet. "We have to be quiet," Essie says, like Juanita is a dumb five-year-old who can't figure this out. It turns out that Victoria won't be back from middle school until a little later. Meanwhile, Víctor is at the college; some part-time coaching has opened up. But he has left his own note posted on the refrigerator.

Essie rolls her eyes as she reads it out loud: " 'Hi, girls. Welcome home. After a snack, please begin your homework.' "

Juanita can't believe that even as a runaway, she's going to be reminded to do her homework!

"But I'm in kindergarten. We don't get any homework." Cari pouts like she's being left out of something fun.

"You're *complaining* that you don't have homework?" Essie looks at her little sister like she'd be too dumb to do homework even if she had some. Then, just like that, Essie tosses the note into the trash can.

"You're not supposed to do that!" Cari heads toward the trash can, but Essie blocks her way. "Victoria hasn't read it!"

"Oh, grow up, Cari! We can tell her what it says. Right, Juanita?"

Juanita doesn't know what to say. She kind of agrees with Cari that you shouldn't throw out a parent's note until your older sister, who is responsible for taking care of you, reads it. But Juanita wants to be part of the grown-up world that Essie is including her in.

"Let's go pick out your bedroom." Essie has grabbed a bunch of cookies and is bounding up the stairs, making a lot of noise for someone who is trying to be quiet so as not to wake up the colonel.

Upstairs, Juanita goes into a tizzy of indecision over which room to pick. Her favorite is the bridal bedroom. But Essie keeps saying she's going to throw up if she stands in it one minute longer. The tropical jungle room is so much like her own room, Juanita would be throwing away a rare opportunity to sleep somewhere different if she chooses it. As for the baseball room, whose glories Essie keeps pitching, it'd be like sleeping in Miguel's room.

Just then Victoria gets home and comes upstairs in search of her sisters. "Where's Papa?" she wants to know. "Didn't he leave a note?" That launches Cari into how Essie threw the note away and wouldn't let her retrieve it from the trash can. Victoria gets all stern and tells Essie that she knows she's not supposed to do that. Soon they are having an argument, just like the ones Juanita and Miguel have. But it's really boring to watch a silly argument when you are not involved in it yourself.

Juanita slips away downstairs, tiptoes past the parlor, sits down quietly at the kitchen table, and begins her homework.

●●●

By suppertime, Tía Lola has joined them. Víctor has some good news to share. It's not yet a hundred percent for sure, but it looks like his part-time coaching job at the college might become full-time.

The Swords cheer. Papa might soon have both a job and a B&B to run! Maybe they won't be starving after all.

"So, are you gonna tell Linda you don't want to be a

44

lawyer anymore?" Essie is talking with her mouth full, but her father is too excited to notice.

"Soon as I have the offer in writing." Papa might not want to be a lawyer, but he still thinks like one, worrying about written proof and stuff. "In fact, I'll be enlisting your help in broadcasting the news."

"What's broadcasting?" Cari wants to know.

"Broadcast is like when you sow seeds." Her father makes a gesture. "Throwing something out there for everyone to see and know."

"Throwing something out," of course, reminds Cari of what Essie did to Papa's note. This is too tempting an opportunity to pass up. Cari blabs. Another argument. This is getting old, Juanita is thinking.

While the Swords argue, Tía Lola and Juanita go upstairs to resolve the sleeping arrangements. Juanita still hasn't decided which room to pick. What does Tía Lola think?

"Let's see. You've got your own tropical room, and your brother's room is a lot like the baseball room. So, really, the most *adventurous* choice would have to be the bridal bedroom." Surely Essie can't look down on that. Adventure would be Essie's middle name if she had one.

"Tía Lola, I'm so glad you've come," Juanita admits, stopping just short of saying that she wishes she were back home in her own bedroom. After making such a big deal about running away, she has to hold out, at least for one night.

At bedtime, Víctor stops by to wish her good night. He apologizes for his daughters' arguing. "Sometimes they can be a pain in the *fundillo,* you know?" Juanita has to agree that the Swords can be a pain in the butt sometimes. "But they're good kids. They'll settle down once they get used to Vermont. Meanwhile, I want to thank you, Juanita. You've been such a help, not to mention a great example."

Juanita's heart swells with pride. Maybe, even if Víctor and Mami end up marrying, Juanita will feel like she does right this moment: loved and appreciated for herself alone. Just this feeling is worth having run away from home for.

❊❊❊

On Friday afternoon, all the children get off the bus in town, including Miguel. Parked in front of Tía Lola's B&B are several cars with out-of-state plates, including a car with New York plates. If only it were Papi's rental car and Juanita had her whole birthday weekend to do all over again!

She takes a deep breath. It's autumn. The air smells like wood fires and minty evergreens. Juanita feels a sudden rush of happiness. Yes, even with her parents divorcing and having to move away from friends like Ming, Juanita is so lucky to be ten and living in a beautiful place with so many new friends and Tía Lola to help with the difficult parts now and then.

Entering through the kitchen door, Juanita hears a familiar voice she can't quite place. Could it be? It's only when she hears the adult voices with their Chinese accents that she is sure! "Ming!" she screams. And then she is running toward the front parlor just as her friend is running into the hallway, screaming back, "Juanita!"

Thank goodness, the colonel has already woken up.

46

Otherwise, he'd think he was back in a battlefield, shouting orders to his men, having to fight some war all over again.

●●●

That night, the two girls are tucked in together in Juanita's canopy bed back in her own bedroom in her very own house.

"This is the coolest bedroom!" Ming has pronounced several times. "If I had a bedroom like this, I'd never run away from home!"

Juanita decides not to remind her friend that it was she, Ming, who recommended running away. But, of course, that was before Ming had come for a visit and seen Juanita's fabulous bedroom.

The lights are off, but there's a soft glow coming in from the hall. Mami has peeked in several times, saying, "Girls, tomorrow's a long day." But the two friends can't help talking into the wee hours. There are so many stories to tell. Ming recounts how her parents finally decided to come up for a visit.

"Your mom called up my mom and told her you were going to run away to New York if I didn't come to see you."

So, it was Mami who thought up this special treat for Juanita! Her birthday has indeed stretched out to a whole second weekend.

"My dad called up your dad for driving directions," Ming goes on. "He also asked for the name of a hotel where we could stay. Your dad told my dad about how Tía Lola had started a wonderful B&B. Except my dad couldn't find it listed anywhere. But there was this other B&B right on your road, so my parents called there."

"Oh no!" Juanita says. "That's Mrs. Beauregard's B&B! She isn't very friendly. I'm so glad you didn't go to her place." Tía Lola's B&B was already full, so they couldn't stay there either. Thank goodness Ming's parents finally accepted Mami's invitation to stay in the farmhouse. This way, the girls could be together.

"But the strange thing is that Mrs. Beau-whatever-her-name-is told my dad that Tía Lola's B&B had been closed down by the authorities."

"That's a lie!" Juanita cries out. Then, remembering that she is supposed to be asleep, she whispers, "It just opened this weekend. And it's already sold out."

"My dad said the owner sounded kind of weird. Anyhow, your mom said for us to meet up in town at Tía Lola's B&B. I'm so glad we finally came to visit."

The two girls go on talking, fighting back sleep because it's so wonderful to be together again.

"There's so much I want to show you," Juanita whispers to Ming. She starts to enumerate all the things they will do tomorrow, including visit Stargazer's store, drop in on Rudy's, explore Colonel Charlebois's attic, maybe even go out to her teacher Mrs. Prouty's horse farm.

By the time she leaves on Sunday, Ming will have fallen in love with Vermont. If she ever needs to run away from home, she will know where to come.

chapter five

How Cari's Kindergarten Teacher
Almost Didn't Get Married

Cari loves her kindergarten teacher. Not just likes, not just is relieved she isn't a mean teacher or a strict teacher, but really la-UH-uvs her nice, curly-red-haired fairy-tale teacher. And what is very special is that her teacher seems to love her back in equal measure!

Every morning Cari wants to bring Ms. McGregor a present. Papa explains that now that he is not working as a lawyer, the family has to budget. Cari will have to think of presents that don't cost money.

With Tía Lola's help, Cari makes an easy-as-pie apple piñata, which Ms. McGregor shares with the whole class. Cari also brings her teacher a bouquet of late-blooming asters from Juanita's flower bed; a pumpkin Miguel grew in a patch in the garden; a discarded candied guinea pig

Tía Lola says looks too much like a skinny rabbit; some shiny buttons from one of Colonel Charlebois's old uniforms that he'd gladly donate to the cause (that's the way he talks); and a pebble that Victoria says is good luck because it has a white ring all the way around it.

But Cari is running out of ideas that don't cost money.

Thank goodness, Tía Lola comes up with a solution: "Why don't you draw whatever you want to give Señorita McGregor and just tell her to use her imagination?"

This is an excellent idea! Cari starts out by drawing a picture of Ms. McGregor holding hands with a little brown girl with dark, straight hair and big brown eyes.

The very day Cari gives Ms. McGregor this special drawing, her teacher makes an announcement to the class: she is getting married. Cari is so excited and claps right along with everyone else.

But a minute later, she's not so sure she is happy about this. If Ms. McGregor gets married, then she'll be busy with Mr. McGregor, or no, wait a minute, she won't even be Ms. McGregor anymore. Cari's not real sure how it works with last names, but she has heard Tía Carmen say that she is probably going to change her name to Guzmán when she marries Miguel and Juanita's *papi*. That way, if they have a baby, Tía Carmen can have the same last name as her child. There's another thing Cari isn't happy about. Ms. McGregor, who might not be Ms. McGregor anymore, could have a baby, and then she'll definitely have her hands full, as everyone knows that you need both hands to hold a baby—or so Cari has been told every time she has been given one to hold.

Every night since she heard about the wedding, Cari has made a wish on a birthday candle that Juanita gave her. It's one of those trick candles that Essie got at Stargazer's store to put on Juanita's cake. You make a wish, then blow and blow, and they don't blow out! Cari assumes that this being a birthday candle, it preserves its wish-granting properties. So, before going to bed, Cari goes in the bathroom with Victoria, who lights it—Papa has given them permission to do this in the bathroom sink only. Then Cari closes her eyes and wishes that Ms. McGregor won't get married. Cari tries blowing out the candle, but it flickers and flares up again, so she gets to make the same wish again and again.

"Wow, that must be some wish," Victoria finally says, startling Cari, who opens her eyes. There is a half-concerned, half-curious look on her big sister's face. Victoria is hinting that she wants to know what all this wishing is about. But Cari can't tell. Wishes have to be kept secret, or they spoil on you. And this is one time when Cari really, really needs for her wish to come true.

❋❋❋

Tía Lola knows all about the wedding, as she is friends with all the teachers at Bridgeport Elementary. It turns out that Maisie (that's Ms. McGregor's first name) is getting married to Boone Magoon, which has to be the silliest name Cari has ever heard! Boone is a young farmer, and since farmers have to milk their cows twice a day every day, the newlyweds can't get away even for a honeymoon weekend. In fact, they're thinking of just having a justice of the peace come out to the farm and marry them on the premises!

So, Tía Lola comes up with a plan. She invites Ms. Mc-Gregor and Mr. Magoon to stay at her B&B at a special newlywed rate. For no extra charge, they can be married right in the elegant front parlor by the colonel himself, who happens to be a justice of the peace. Since they'll be in town, Boone can still milk his cows in the morning, attend his own wedding in the afternoon, then go out for the evening milking and be back again for a honeymoon night. Ms. McGregor is delighted and accepts right off.

Normally, Cari would love for someone special to be staying at their B&B. It's like having a sleepover. But Cari doesn't want her teacher to get married. So having Ms. McGregor stay for her honeymoon at Tía Lola's B&B will be like hitting herself on a boo-boo and having it start to bleed all over again.

Every time the topic of the wedding comes up, Cari pouts. "But I thought you'd be excited." Papa is puzzled. He is happily preparing the rooms for the wedding party. (Ms. McGregor's parents are driving over from Maine; her sister is flying in from L.A.) The couple will, of course, be given the bridal bedroom. "What an enlightened idea it was to decorate the room this way," Papa exclaims. Victoria gives him a little I-told-you-so smile but nicely doesn't say so out loud. "Wasn't that a brilliant idea of your big sister's?" Papa adds, trying to pull the sullen Cari into the conversation.

"I think it's stupid! Stupid idea. Stupid room. Stupid, stupid, stupid!" Cari has run out of things to call stupid, which makes her feel really stupid. On top of which, Papa gives Cari a little scolding about not-nice responses, then sends her up to her room for some time out, and that is the stupidest thing of all.

● ● ●

Early in the week, Ms. McGregor comes over to Tía Lola's B&B to finalize the arrangements. She brings along some blank invitations she bought at Stargazer's store. Victoria, whose handwriting is really pretty, has agreed to help her fill them out. Meanwhile, Papa, who has atrocious handwriting but is great at licking envelopes, seals them up. The rest of the crew heads upstairs to clean the rooms and make a list of supplies needed.

The only people coming to the ceremony in the colonel's front parlor will be the groom's family, Ms. Mc-Gregor's parents and sister, the Espadas, the Guzmáns, and of course, Tía Lola. But Rudy has thrown open his restaurant for a party afterward. Instead of gifts, the couple requests that guests bring their favorite family dish with the recipe written down. After all, no one was even expecting to be invited to a last-minute wedding that would have taken place in a stable among a hundred head of Holsteins and Jerseys if Tía Lola hadn't come to the rescue.

The last invitation Victoria addresses is for the Magoon family, not that they need one. But Ms. McGregor says it's for his parents and sister to have as a keepsake. It turns out Boone's father can't farm anymore on account of his bad arthritis, and his sister is confined to a wheelchair from a car accident. Meanwhile, his mother is kept busy taking care of them both. All of these details Victoria learns from Ms. McGregor as they work together at the kitchen table.

53

Victoria can't help sighing. These young lovers have fallen in love amid such sad circumstances, like the star-crossed Romeo and Juliet. How wonderful that Tía Lola thought up a special wedding package. Victoria puts extra flourish into the handwritten details of where and when the ceremony will take place and the ensuing reception. Before giving Papa the invitation to seal, Victoria sprays the card with the rose-scented air freshener she bought for the bridal bedroom.

"Where's one of my favorite kindergartners?" Ms. Mc-Gregor keeps asking. It is odd that Cari hasn't come down to say hi to her beloved teacher. On several occasions, Papa calls up the stairs. But Cari is sitting in the front parlor, listening to Colonel Charlebois snore in his rocking chair. Finally, when the cleaning crew comes downstairs, all finished with their work, and no Cari is along, Papa goes in search of her. He spots her, crouched by the dark fireplace, holding on to Valentino as if he were her life raft.

Papa motions for her to come out to the hall so as not to wake the colonel. "Caridad Espada, I've been calling and calling you. Why don't you answer?" Papa never calls her by her full name unless he means business.

Cari shrugs. She doesn't answer because she doesn't want to go into the kitchen and hear about her kinder-garten teacher's stupid wedding all over again. That's like having a boo-boo, bruising it once, and then bruising it a second time. How's it ever supposed to feel better if she keeps bumping up against this wedding everywhere she turns, even when she comes home from school?

"A shrug is not an admissible reply," Papa says in his

lawyer voice. But then, in his nicer Papa voice, he adds, "It's Ms. McGregor, your favorite teacher, remember? Don't you want to come say hi to her?"

Cari shakes her head. "I don't want to go in the stupid kitchen."

"I think there's been far too much use of the word 'stupid' in the last few days," Papa says, his lawyer voice back. "I think it's time we put a moratorium on the word 'stupid' and try to come up with nicer ways of expressing what ails us."

Cari doesn't know what a "morontorium" is. But she's not going to ask Papa to explain, because if she opens her mouth, she will burst out crying.

After getting that big word out of his system, Papa comes down on his knees so he's eye level with Cari. His face is full of concern. "I know something's bugging you, Cari Cakes. But how can I or your sisters or Tía Lola or Ms. McGregor help you if you won't tell us what's wrong?"

Valentino ambles over and licks Cari's hand. He wants to be included on the list of those willing to help Cari with whatever is upsetting her.

Cari's head is bowed so low, her chin is almost touching her neck.

Papa hesitates, and then in a sad voice, he asks, "Is it that you don't like Vermont? That you want to go back to Queens?"

Oh no, that's not it at all. Cari shakes her head. She never wants to go back to Queens. She loves Vermont. She loves kindergarten. She just doesn't want anything to change. When things change, it can get scary and sad. Like when their mother died, even though Cari doesn't really remember. Or when Lupita, her beloved babysitter back in Queens, moved away to North Carolina because she also was getting married, to someone in the military.

Just thinking of all these sad changes, Cari starts sobbing so hard, her father has to wait until Cari calms down so he can make out what she is saying.

"I just don't want Ms. McGregor to get married. I want her to be my teacher forever. I don't want to call her Mrs. Magoon."

Instead of consoling her, Papa is laughing!

"You said to tell so you could help. It's not nice to laugh."

"I'm not laughing at you, Cakes. But here's the honest truth: sometimes there's just nothing we can do to stop change from happening." Papa's voice suddenly sounds a little wistful. "The good news is that time is a great healer of boo-boos great and small. Helping others is also a big help when we're sad. So, what do you say you come out to the kitchen and help us out?"

Cari enters the kitchen sheepishly, hidden behind Papa's legs. Everyone gives her a rousing welcome, as if she has been around the world and just got back, safe and sound. Ms. McGregor even swoops down for a big hug. Then Papa gives Cari her very own job: polishing a velvet-lined box of tarnished silverware that the colonel hasn't used since he was a boy in his mother's house. In case Rudy needs extras, it's good to be prepared.

"Cari is excellent with silverware," her father brags. He sets her up with a rag and a big jar of polish at one end

of the long table. At the other end, Victoria and Ms. Mc-
Gregor are finishing up the invitations. Cari is amazed
how much fun it is, rubbing and rubbing the dusky forks
and spoons and knives, like Aladdin with his magic lamp.
When Cari finishes the last spoon, she holds it up, and like
a fun-house mirror, she sees her brooooooooad brown
face smiling stupidly back at her.

❋❋❋

Friday, when Cari gets home with Essie on the bus, they
find Colonel Charlebois napping in the parlor. Papa is
gone and Victoria's not yet back from her slightly longer
school day. But there is a note on the refrigerator that
Essie reads out loud: " 'Hey, B&B crew. Out coaching. You
know what to do! Be back by six. Love, Papa.' "

"What do you think Papa wants us to do?" Cari asks
Essie.

Her sister shrugs. "Do our homework—what else?"

"I don't get homework in kindergarten." Cari has to
keep reminding everyone. Maybe people who get homework don't get any smarter.

"Hello?! It's also Friday! Papa's just in one of his states,"
Essie pronounces in a grown-up voice. "He's so happy
coaching, he's like a kid in a candy store."

"Do you think he'll ever be a lawyer again?" Cari
knows that was Papa's job in the city. But here in Vermont,
Papa has changed his mind about what he wants to be as a
grown-up. That's a change that could be scary, but somehow it isn't. Cari isn't sure why.

"No way Papa's going to be a lawyer anymore. He de-
tests being a lawyer." Now that Essie is in sixth grade, she

57

has begun using an awful lot of big words. "Besides, Papa loves coaching and helping run Tía Lola's B&B. I haven't seen Papa this happy since—I don't know, since . . ." And then Essie blurts out the one comparison she has been avoiding: "Since before Mama died."

Suddenly Cari understands why all the recent changes haven't been scary: because they've made Papa so happy, it makes everyone else feel happy, too. So maybe when Ms. McGregor gets married, she and her husband will be so happy, there will be a lot of leftover happiness for them to give everybody, including Cari. She's not sure why, but somehow over the last few days, being so occupied polishing silver and helping Papa, and seeing Ms. McGregor so excited at school, Cari has stopped moping. At night, Victoria has to remind her about the wishing candle. But Cari is all done with wishing her teacher won't get married.

"Your turn," she tells Victoria. "You wish for something."

●●●

It is Saturday afternoon, and the wedding guests are assembled in the front parlor.

The big grandfather clock clangs three o'clock. Then ticks to three-ten, quarter after. The guests grow restless.

Upstairs, the bride is pacing her bedroom, trampling rose petals underfoot. "Where is he?" she keeps asking no one in particular. Periodically she sends her little flower girl down to check on the arrival of the groom and his family.

Every time Cari races back upstairs with the news that there is no news, she dreads seeing the unhappiness on

58

her teacher's face. It is a face Cari knows by heart after a month in kindergarten. Ms. McGregor is looking even more unhappy than when she has to remind Leo Pellegrini for the fourth time in one morning that he has to raise his hand and wait to be called on before he can have a turn at talking.

Finally Ms. McGregor marches down to the kitchen to call her husband-to-be and remind him that he is getting married this afternoon. But nobody answers at his house, and he doesn't have a machine, so Ms. McGregor can't leave a message.

"Maybe there has been an emergency, you think?" Papa ventures. After all, with a sickly father and a sister in a wheelchair, anything could happen.

"He could at least call and tell us so," the bride says with a temper that Cari has never heard in her teacher's voice before.

"I just can't believe he doesn't have a cell," her sister says, shaking her head in disbelief. That should have been a red flag right there. Everyone in L.A. has a cell.

"I'm really sorry." Ms. McGregor is apologizing like it's her fault. "I guess he wasn't ready to marry me." Her voice breaks. Tears are streaming down her beautiful face.

Cari is feeling so guilty. She knows who is responsible, and it's not the groom. It's Caridad Espada, who spent a week wishing on a non-quitting candle that her teacher wouldn't get married. And even though, in the last few days, she has stopped wishing this, it was probably too late for the wish fairies. They already had it in the works, Ms. McGregor will not be getting married.

Cari can't bear one more minute of watching the consequences of her selfishness. She lets herself out of the house without a coat and sits down on the front steps, shivering in her thin party dress with her little crown of silk roses. Maybe she will die of poohmonia, or whatever it's called. Before she knows it, Cari is blubbering away herself, not caring that all the traffic coming into town gets to see her being a big baby.

Such is her despair, eyes clouded with tears, that Cari hears before she sees the huge red pickup with a wheelchair in the back pulling up onto the front lawn. A young man is leaping out from behind the wheel, leaving the other passengers inside. He's holding a white envelope and breathing in a rushed way, like he might have a heart attack before Cari ever finds out why he's so upset. "Is this where the wedding is? Is Maisie here? Maisie McGregor?"

Cari pops right up. "Yes! Yes!" She races down the last couple of steps and grabs the groom's hand. Together, they rush into the house, the man hollering over his shoulder, "I'll be right back soon's I explain!"

It is an astonishing moment Cari will never forget: the groom bursting into the kitchen, looking sick with worry; a teary Ms. McGregor standing up, half relieved, half mad, and another half that Cari can't know adds up to more than a whole because she hasn't learned fractions yet—that other extra half ready to cancel the wedding even if it kills her, which it would: all three halves of her dying of a broken heart.

The groom doesn't even try to explain. He hurries over and folds his bride in his arms, kissing the tears away.

60

Everyone tiptoes out so that the young lovers can have their private moment of making up. Everyone except one wedding-party dog with a white satin ribbon round his neck and a little flower girl who stays to keep him company under the kitchen table.

Later, when the whole story is told, the question will remain: who changed the address on the groom's family's invitation? Right now what Cari learns is that Boone's family got the invitation, but the address it gave was not Colonel Charlebois's house in town, but an address out in the country. (He shows Ms. McGregor the invitation as proof.) Boone figured he'd misunderstood, and the wedding was actually out at the colonel's old place. So he drove to the address on the invitation: a ramshackle, unpainted house with a B&B sign on the front lawn. He knocked and knocked. Nobody answered. By now it was almost three in the afternoon, and he was in a panic. He didn't have a cell phone, so he couldn't call Colonel Charlebois to see where the heck he should go. He decided to just drive through town, hoping and praying that he'd spot a house with lots of parked cars that might signal a wedding party.

"Then, remember that cute picture you showed me by one of your students, a pretty little girl holding your hand? Well, I saw that same little girl in a party dress with a flower crown sitting in front of this house, so I pulled in. And sure enough, she said you were inside." He lets out a long sigh. "You will still marry me, won't you? Maisie, please?"

Before Ms. McGregor can refuse him, Cari jumps out from under the table. "Say yes, Ms. McGregor, please. It's all my fault for wishing you wouldn't marry!"

Both the bride and groom are rendered momentarily speechless by this outburst from an unexpected witness. Then her teacher's face relaxes into a soft smile. "It's not your fault, Cari. Look, he's right." Ms. McGregor shows Cari the invitation, forgetting that Cari is in kindergarten and can't read handwriting. But she does know what her big sister's handwriting looks like, and the writing on that card is definitely not Victoria's. It looks like someone painted over a mistake and wrote on the whited-out part with a fine-point marker.

Ms. McGregor kisses Cari and thanks her for delivering her groom safely to her side. "Now let's get this wedding over and done with before the cows start coming home to be milked!"

The groom goes out to fetch his family from the pickup and take them to the front parlor. Meanwhile, upstairs in her bedroom, the bride finishes touching up her makeup just as Tía Lola climbs the stairs to announce that it is time. Actually, it is way over time, but everyone has forgotten the blip in the happiness of the moment. Except for Tía Lola, who has looked over that whited-out address and suspects who might have wanted to ruin her B&B's first wedding weekend.

"You ready?" Tía Lola asks the young bride, who smiles radiantly in reply.

Then Ms. McGregor, who will soon be Mrs. Magoon, kisses her sister and reaches for Cari's hand and squeezes it. "We are ready, right?"

Cari nods. She is ready to let her teacher become Mr. Magoon's wife.

chapter six

How Victoria Got Her Wish and Wished She Hadn't

Oh my goodness! Victoria cannot believe what wishing on an old birthday candle—just to indulge a little sister—has brought about.

All she wished for was that a family with one cute teenage boy would come to stay at Tía Lola's B&B.

Up pulls a van with a college name and logo on the side door. Out jump not one, not two, not even five, but seven guys, eight counting their coach. This must be the water polo team Papa got a call from last night. The coach hadn't been able to find accommodations for all fifteen team members, so he called the home coach, who happened to know about a B&B that had just opened. Maybe it had some vacancies.

Victoria hadn't been paying any attention when the call came through. She had just gotten off the phone with

Melanie, one of her new girlfriends, who was sobbing because her eighth-grade crush had asked another seventh grader to go to the movies. In other words, Victoria was in the middle of an emotional emergency-room situation, and here was Papa pacing and gesturing for Victoria to get off the phone.

Life in the seventh grade is turning out to have a lot of these crisis moments—for her girlfriends, that is. Victoria herself is not allowed to date, and when she tries to pin Papa down on when he'll lift the ban, her father gets very vague about there being plenty of time for that in the future.

No wonder Victoria has resorted to wishing on other people's birthday candles for B&B guests with teenage sons! It's pathetic, if you ask her. Which Papa won't. The only benefit to being out of the dating game is that every seventh-grade girl with a heartache ends up confiding in Victoria. But then, the one way she can fit in, Papa also ruins by establishing the five-minute-phone-call rule.

Last night with Melanie, Victoria knew she had gone way over this limit. And she would be hearing all about it as soon as she got off the phone. Her father would start in on this being Colonel Charlebois's house (not that the sweet old man cares a hoot about Victoria's being on the phone) and how, now that Victoria is going to be thirteen, she really needs to show more consideration.

But no sooner had Victoria put the phone down than it rang again. Papa picked it up, and instead of saying, "Oh, hi, Melanie," he said, "This is he." Victoria sprinted upstairs so that when Papa concluded his call and came up to

64

have a word with her, he'd find his eldest fast at work on an assignment, which he wouldn't want to interrupt. Papa is big on his daughters doing their homework.

But Papa didn't come up. Victoria could hear him on the second floor getting the rooms ready. She thought of going down to help out but decided that she'd be asking for it. Instead, she got the story secondhand from Cari, who mixed up the details: some water polo team coaches were coming for a meeting. (Cari thought a meet and a meeting were the same thing.) Victoria pictured a bunch of old guys with beer bellies telling corny jokes she would have to pretend were funny.

Quickly, as the guys are now at the door, Victoria slips into the bathroom to check on her hair. She also wants to be sure her jaw is hinged back in place so she doesn't go downstairs to welcome this weekend's B&B guests looking like she never saw a boy before in her life.

As she descends the stairs, Victoria has a view of the parlor. Colonel Charlebois is snoring away, which is incredible considering the commotion in the front hall. For a second, Victoria's thoughts turn to the old man. Several times recently, Tía Lola has mentioned that she is concerned about Colonel Charlebois. He has been sleeping too much. Like maybe he is depressed or sick or taking too many pills or something.

Just inside the mudroom, Essie has already launched into her welcome routine. "Tía Lola's historic B&B was founded by a direct descendant of Christopher Columbus." If Papa could hear her! He'd launch into his own routine about historical accuracy. Of course, Essie would argue that Tía Lola comes from the Dominican Republic, which is where Christopher Columbus first landed, and Tía Lola herself has said that almost everyone on the island is her cousin.

"Hey, hey, hey!" One of the guys has caught sight of Victoria. He has curly brown hair and a mischievous grin. "And who is this?"

"That's my sister," Essie says, as if pointing out the bathroom.

"Yo there, big sister!" the same guy says. He sure is a bigmouth. Maybe he's the captain or something.

"My dad's coaching soccer, but he'll be back by supper," Essie rattles on. "He said to make yourselves at home. We have three guest rooms and air mattresses and stuff. We also have some more space in the attic, if you need it."

"You guys can have my room," Victoria blurts out, and the next moment her cheeks are burning, as she sounded so eager. "I can sleep in my little sister's room," she adds more evenly.

"How about your bedroom with you in it?" The same guy again. His teammates erupt in laughter. Excuse me? That was funny?

"Out of line, Cohen," the coach barks. "You owe the young lady an apology."

Cohen bows his curly head and mutters something, maybe an apology. But the harm's done. All his buddies are looking her over like she's some menu they're going to order from. Victoria feels mortified. Until this moment, she had no idea what reserves of courage it took to face

66

seven college guys without looking like an animal surprised in the headlights of a car.

When the phone rings and it's Melanie, Victoria somehow gets back into the groove of being excited about her wish come true. "That's right, seven. They're doubling up. The coach and another guy are taking my room."

"You are *so* lucky!" Melanie sighs. "I wish my parents had a B&B."

"I know," Victoria agrees. But what she really wants to say is *Be careful what you wish for!* Another insight of this eye-opening day: a lot of good luck is in the eye of the beholder.

✹✹✹

Friday night, the water polo team takes off to practice and get acquainted with the college pool. Papa asks if he can tag along, and Miguel and Essie go with him. That leaves Victoria and Tía Lola and Linda and the younger girls to play dominoes with the colonel in the front parlor. They chat and sip a ginger tea Tía Lola made especially for Colonel Charlebois.

"Mmm, tastes good." The colonel nods appreciatively. "Much better than my usual brew." All day he sips tea from the thermos his cleaning girl prepares for him.

Tonight, he seems quite lively. Maybe that's all the old man has been missing? Some attention? Tía Lola certainly hopes so. She wants to get to the bottom of why the colonel has been so tired recently. She feels responsible for this B&B idea. Maybe Linda was right to begin with, and all this added commotion has been too much for the old man. If so, Tía Lola is ready to close down her B&B, rather than risk the colonel's good health and sanity.

The phone keeps ringing—that alone could drive anyone crazy. The calls are always for Victoria. Although she has told only Melanie about the water polo team, Melanie can't keep her mouth shut, and soon most of their mutual girlfriends are calling Victoria to confirm the story.

"Sorry about that," Victoria says after the last call.

"You certainly are a popular gal," the colonel notes gallantly. "I feel very honored that you have a free night to spend with us."

"They're just girlfriends." Victoria doesn't mean to make her girlfriends sound like second-class citizens. It's just that her calls are definitely not romantic, as the colonel probably imagines. "I'm not allowed to date," she adds, making a face.

"Date?!" Linda looks shocked. "Don't tell me seventh graders are now dating?"

"Except for Victoria Espada," Victoria says with grievance in her voice. One more thing that sets her apart, along with being the only one of her friends whose mother has died, and the only kid with brown skin in her whole class—it turns out that it's exotic to be Hispanic in Vermont. Add to that a strict papa who thinks dating is only for the middle-aged (like for him and Linda), and Victoria doesn't stand a chance of being like everybody else.

Linda looks over at her daughter. "Don't you go getting any ideas, Juana Inés!"

"Maaaami!" Juanita wails. "I'm only in fourth grade! Besides, who'd want to date a yuckety-yuck boy, anyway?"

"Yuckety-yuck, yuckety-yuck." Cari sways her head left and right to the rollicking sound.

"Apparently, you both will when you're seventh graders," Mami says, sighing. But then, wanting Victoria to feel she can confide in her father's new girlfriend, Linda adds, "Would you really like to be able to date?"

Victoria isn't sure if it's the dating she misses or not being able to do the things her friends do. What if she could date and this Cohen guy asked her out? Yuckety-yuck is right.

"If I were a young man again, I know who I'd be asking out," the colonel says with a twinkle in his eye. Victoria flashes him a grateful smile. She can't explain it, but when the colonel pays her a compliment, she feels so special, as compared to the crude come-on of that Cohen guy.

"But alas"—the colonel takes a deep sigh—"those days are behind me."

Tía Lola's forehead creases with concern. "How *are* you feeling these days, Colonel Charlebois? You don't seem yourself."

"Don't you start fussing over me," the colonel says gruffly, but you can tell he is touched by Tía Lola's concern. "I'm just a little tired lately, that's all. And no, it has nothing to do with your B&B or my wonderful new housemates. I suppose now that baseball season is over, there's not much for me to do. I sit around all day and nod off. I try to read, but my eyes have gotten so bad."

"I've got an idea," Victoria pipes up. She has been feeling pangs of shame. It's well into her second month in the colonel's house, and she can't remember the last time

69

she sat down to visit with the old man. He's just been so easy to overlook in all the hectic excitement of their move to a new town, a new school, new friends, the B&B, babysitting for her little sisters. But that's no reason to ignore him. "How about if I read to you a little every day? Maybe the newspaper or a history book." Her father would love that. He is big on his daughters knowing the deeds of the past.

"That is a lovely offer, my dear." The colonel's eyes have gone all misty. "But you are a busy young lady."

"No, I'm not!" Victoria says with surprising determination. Her father has often noted that his sweet, pliant eldest has a will of steel once she decides on a certain course. "And this way, I can learn all about the great deeds of the past and stuff." The offer itself is genuine, but the follow-up is baloney, and the colonel knows the difference. "Really, it'll be fun," Victoria adds with convincing warmth.

"Okay, we've got a date. But on two conditions: First, I pay for this reading service. Second, I've had enough history in my life. I think a little romantic fiction would do me some good, or maybe that Harry Potter fellow." The colonel winks at Victoria. "Who knows?" he adds, looking over at Tía Lola. "Between your ginger teas and your readings"—he nods to each lovely lady—"I'll be dancing merengue by Christmas!"

When the phone rings again, Victoria hurries to answer it. But it turns out to be for Colonel Charlebois. "Your cleaning girl," Victoria says, reentering the room.

The colonel gets up grumpily. He has already told the teenage girl that he doesn't need her to clean the whole house anymore. The Espada family has insisted on doing the housework as a way of compensating the colonel for not charging them rent. Needless to say, the girl is not pleased. "My mother's going to kill me if I lose this job," she has reportedly told him. Partly to help her out, and also because deep down the gruff old man is a sweetheart, the colonel has kept her on part-time to do his washing and ironing, attend to his things, etc. She slips in and out so quietly, no one but Papa and Colonel Charlebois have laid eyes on her.

Out on the hall phone, the colonel sounds like he's finalizing arrangements for tomorrow's cleaning. "Okay then, Miss Beauregard. My regards to your mother."

Tía Lola jumps as if she just sat down on Essie's whoopee cushion, a gag that Victoria's sister thinks is so hilarious. Victoria means to ask Tía Lola what's up, but just as the colonel hangs up, the phone rings again. "Oh, good evening, Melanie," he is saying. "Let me see if she is available."

● ● ●

Saturday morning, after sleeping in, the water polo team comes down noisily to breakfast. They wolf down their pancakes, laughing loudly, tossing their napkins across the table at each other. They're like puppies, Victoria thinks, but even Valentino was better behaved when he was a pup.

The team has a few hours to kill before their game this afternoon. "Any hot spots in town we should take in?" Cohen asks Victoria, arching an eyebrow suggestively, as if she knows what he means. Just to be a pill, Victoria tells him that there's a great military museum across the lake at Fort Ticonderoga. "You'll learn a lot of American history

71

and stuff there. Really," she adds because the guy is looking at her like she just dropped in from outer space.

He snorts and looks over at his friends, who snort back. They sound like a bunch of hogs. "You got to be kidding," he says at last.

"Victoria is absolutely right," her father chimes in. He is surprised by his eldest's recommendation, as Victoria has never shown a particular liking for history. But now that she's almost thirteen, her tastes are maturing, no doubt. "It's well worth your while."

Hog Cohen snorts again. "I'd rather make history than learn about it, you know?" He grins at Victoria, watching for her reaction. It's as if he gets a real kick out of embarrassing her.

The team takes off, leaving their duffel bags of equipment in the front hall where they dropped them off after last night's practice. Victoria has to navigate her way through that obstacle course as she heads for the parlor to keep her promise and read to the colonel. She trips over a bulky bag sticking out from the others—probably Cohen's. Victoria can't help herself. She whacks it with her foot, once, twice, six, seven times. And one more for good measure. She had no idea guys could be so rude and in your face. If this is what she'd be dating, Victoria will gladly wait till middle age.

❁❁❁

Melanie, along with two other friends, Sophie and Emily, drop by just as the water polo team is returning to pick up their gear. Cohen invites the girls to come watch the game. "Just as long as you cheer for us, deal?"

The girls giggle assent. Honestly. Victoria is feeling increasingly frustrated with her silly friends. All they seem to think about is boys. If this is what dating does to the human brain, who needs it?

Victoria would just as soon pass on going to the game, but Papa is off coaching, and so she has to babysit her sisters, who've also been invited to the game. Essie would have a major meltdown if Victoria proposed staying at home instead. Besides, Tía Lola is coming along with Juanita and Miguel, which should make it fun. And most importantly, the colonel is eager to go. It'll do him good to be out and about.

"I'd have you know the last water polo game I watched was the famous Blood in the Water match," the colonel informs the team. "Summer Olympics, 1956, Hungarians against the Soviets." The colonel goes on to describe the historic game. Amazingly, the young teammates are hanging on his every word. Even Cohen is listening. Certain kinds of history must be okay to learn about. Victoria can't help noticing the absorbed, almost sweet expression on the team captain's face. Maybe when he finally grows up, Cohen will turn into a nice human being whom Victoria might consider dating.

●●●

It's time for the game to start. The home team has already been out swimming laps for a good fifteen minutes. Her friends are gossiping away, so they don't seem to notice the delay, but Victoria is growing restless. Where is the visiting team?

Finally their coach comes out and confers with the

home coach, who shakes his head and accompanies him into the locker room. He comes back out and makes an announcement. The visiting team will need another fifteen minutes. There is some problem with their equipment.

Of course, the first thing that comes into Victoria's mind is that series of walloping kicks she delivered to the clunky sports bag. What if she broke some critical piece of equipment? She feels awful. She'll have to fess up. Victoria wouldn't sink so low as to do something wrong and then be a sneak about it. But this is just the kind of ammunition she does not want to give a guy like Cohen.

When the visiting team finally trots out of the locker room, Victoria is so relieved, she stands up and screams right along with her friends. Thank goodness, nobody's wearing something broken and patched up. In fact, they're hardly wearing anything at all, except caps and teensy striped Speedos that look like they can easily be yanked off. And they can be, as evidenced several times in the course of the ensuing game. Victoria doesn't know where to look, and neither do her friends. "That's disgusting," Melanie mutters. "Yuck!" Emily agrees. "Double yuck," Sophie adds. Another source of relief for Victoria. Maybe she's not so different from her girlfriends after all.

♦♦♦

When the team comes back to check out from Tía Lola's B&B, Victoria and Melanie join everyone in the hall to congratulate them on their win. The minute Cohen and his teammates spot Victoria, they turn angrily on her.

"Thanks a lot," Cohen spits out. "What a mean, double-crossing . . ." This time, the coach doesn't tell him that he's out of order.

Victoria's eyes burn. It's her turn to mutter: "I'm sorry. I didn't mean to ruin anything."

"Well, you did! If we hadn't won the match, I would've wrung—"

"Out of order, Cohen," the coach barks. "It was a silly prank but not grounds for murder."

"It wasn't a prank," Victoria says, sniffling, and struggling to keep tears from spilling. She doesn't want to cry in front of seven guys, one coach, her sisters, and her new friends. "I just was mad with all these bags in the way. I didn't mean to break anything. It was just a kick. A little kick." She demonstrates, a less vigorous version of the original whacks she gave his bag.

"What are you talking about?" Cohen narrows his eyes, as if he can see right through Victoria. "Don't try to cover up how you smeared Vaseline all over our equipment."

"Smeared Vaseline?" Victoria's sobs immediately stop. It's as if Cohen has uttered the magic words that control her tear ducts. This is no time to be a crybaby. She has her defense to mount. "I would *never* do such a mean thing."

Cohen's upper lip curls cynically. He shakes his head. He knows better. "You've had this thing against us from the get-go."

The colonel steps forward, ready to do battle for the fair Victoria. "How dare you impugn the honor of a lady!" he thunders, wagging a finger at the surprised young man. "You owe her an apology."

The coach intervenes. "Let me get this straight. None of you put Vaseline all over the gear in our bags?"

"No one here would do such a thing," the colonel declares indignantly. "And I can vouch that no one came into this house except those present and their parents, so help me God. And I have proudly worn the uniform of the United States Army for longer than any of you have been around."

Tía Lola has been listening keenly to the conversation. Just now when the colonel vouched that no one had come into the house except those present and Víctor and Linda, he was forgetting one other person. The cleaning girl with the same last name as someone who seems to be bent on destroying the reputation of Tía Lola's B&B. But one thing Tía Lola loves about her new country is how everyone is innocent until proven guilty. She will not blame anyone until she has some evidence. But from now on, she will keep her eyes wide open.

"I've been, like, a total jerk, and I'm sorry." Cohen is apologizing? "And you know what bugged me most of all? I just couldn't get my head around how an awesome girl like you would, like, do such a crappy thing."

"Language," the coach barks. "You're talking to a lady."

A lady, an awesome girl. Oh my goodness! Victoria feels a thrilling rush. If she were to go back to that candle stub, this moment is all she would wish for.

By evening, the team has left with many thanks to Tía Lola and her hardworking crew. Even though the mystery of the Vaseline prank is still unsolved, the coach assures Tía Lola that he'll be recommending her B&B to all his colleagues and friends.

The house is quiet again. Victoria and her sisters strip the beds and clean up the guest rooms with help from Juanita and Tía Lola and Miguel. At one point, Victoria peeks in on the colonel. He has dozed off, but this evening, it's understandable that he would be tired after his outing. She tiptoes in and collects his empty cup and lifts the tea thermos he always has by his side. It needs a refill. Before she exits into the kitchen, Victoria has no idea what gets into her. She leans over and kisses the old man on the forehead. Let her friends date all the seventh and eighth graders they want. For now she'll stick to a guy who has already grown up into a gentle old man.

chapter seven

How the Mystery of the B&B Mishaps
Became Even More Mysterious

Tía Lola is determined to solve the mystery of all the mishaps that have been happening at her B&B. But since she's not at the colonel's house full-time, she needs someone in residence to keep an eye out.

It's not difficult to decide whom to pick. Esperanza Espada is curious. She loves adventure. Perhaps even more than Valentino, Essie has the nose of a hound.

Tía Lola decides to include Miguel in her confidence. After all, he was the one who saved the guinea-pig weekend from total disaster. And even policemen work in pairs. Miguel and Essie will make the perfect team for getting to the bottom of the mysterious B&B mishaps.

So, one night when the Espadas are over for dinner, Tía Lola invites Essie up to her room. She gestures to Miguel to follow. Valentino, who likes to be included in any project involving possible treats, trots up behind them.

Tía Lola closes her bedroom door, then checks her closet and under her bed. Both kids are ready to jump out of their skin with nervous excitement. Valentino watches. But once it's clear that no treats are involved, he lies down by the door and dozes off.

"As you know, there have been a series of unfortunate mishaps at my B&B," Tía Lola begins. And then she enumerates them: the locked house the first night of the guinea-pig weekend, the forged change of address on the McGregor–Magoon wedding invitation, the harmful rumor about the authorities closing down Tía Lola's B&B, the Vaseline smeared all over the water polo team's gear. Both Essie and Miguel had noticed one or another of these mishaps, but now, all bunched together, they have to agree with Tía Lola that something fishy is going on.

"Do you . . . I mean, is the house haunted, you think?" A shiver goes up Essie's spine. "It *is* an old house," she says defensively, because Miguel is looking at her like she is a little baby who believes in witches and ghosts and maybe even the tooth fairy.

"The house *is* haunted." Tía Lola confirms Essie's fears but then adds, "Haunted by a real living person."

"You mean, like, by a criminal?" Essie swallows the lump in her throat. A real-life burglar or murderer is a lot more scary than a ghost. After all, if the game of rock-paper-scissors were played with ghost-murderer-burglar, the murderer would win hands down, as murderers create ghosts by killing people, including burglars!

"Whoever it is might not think they're a criminal, but they are doing wrong things. I need your help in finding out who it is."

Miguel is quick to volunteer. Of course, it's not his house being targeted. Still, Essie has a reputation to uphold. "Sure, Tía Lola, but can I also ask Colonel Charlebois to help us?" He has been a soldier all his life, with a chest full of medals. Essie would feel a lot better with the colonel covering her back.

Tía Lola shakes her head firmly. She is very sure the colonel should not be involved. She is worried about him. He hasn't been himself lately, sleeping so much, sluggish and tired all the time. He claims that this change has nothing to do with her B&B. But Tía Lola suspects that there is a connection. After all, it was only after her B&B opened that the colonel started sleeping all the time. "Unless we solve this mystery, I'm afraid we will have to close down Tía Lola's B&B."

The children groan at this terrible news. The B&B is the one really fun thing they were counting on this long winter.

Seeing their unhappy faces, Tía Lola tries to cheer them up. "Maybe we can solve the mystery, and all will be well. So, I want you to keep your eyes open."

"I can't when I'm asleep." Essie doesn't want to sound contrary, but it's a well-known fact that criminals as well as ghosts prefer to do their business late at night.

"That's where Valentino comes in. Right, Valentino?"

Valentino has been dreaming that he is chasing a rabbit. But before he can catch it, someone calls his name. He shakes himself awake, just in time to hear himself pronounced the official night watchdog at Tía Lola's B&B.

He barks, accepting. He can catch up on his sleep during the day with the colonel and prowl the house at night for treats that need to be confiscated before they spoil at daybreak.

●●●

From feeling initially trembly, Essie shifts into high detective gear. She asks to borrow Colonel Charlebois's magnifying glass, which he uses for sorting his collection of stamps and coins from around the world. Essie also buys a little notebook at Stargazer's shop to jot down interesting suspicious stuff: like Papa and Linda whispering something about "telling the children," or the chips mysteriously disappearing from the bowl left on the kitchen counter overnight. (Valentino hangs his head sheepishly.) Or what about Victoria and Colonel Charlebois both conked out in the parlor, their little teacups side by side on the card table, and the Harry Potter book Victoria was reading fallen on the floor, suspiciously opened to the chapter "Halloween."

"Very, very in-ter-es-ting," Essie keeps muttering. It has become what her father calls her "mantra."

"What's a man trap?" Cari asks, looking around warily.

"A man-tra," Papa pronounces. "It's like a chant that people of certain religions repeat when they are praying."

Cari looks relieved, and so does Essie. Her father has been momentarily distracted from wondering what mischief his second oldest is up to.

Both Miguel and Tía Lola have told Essie that she

needs to be less obvious. Walking around on tiptoe with a magnifying glass, a little notebook, and a whistle around her neck is bound to draw attention to their secret investigation.

Also, parents can be distracted from asking about suspicious behavior only for so long. "Care to clue us in as to what is going on?" her father asks when he finds Essie investigating the coat closet with her flashlight.

"I'm working on a project," Essie tells her father. It's the truth, sort of. Of course, Papa assumes Essie means a school project, as in homework, as in *Good for you, Essie, for buckling down*. Essie suspects that detectives have to be granted a license to tell many white lies.

The only person who is downright annoyed with Essie's sleuthing is the colonel's cleaning girl. It's funny how before now, Essie hardly ever noticed Henny. She usually comes when the Swords are at school. But even when the girls are home, Henny slips in so quietly to clean the colonel's room and do his laundry and put out his tea tray and medication that the colonel himself doesn't always notice her. Of course, he's sound asleep half of the time.

Henny isn't exactly the kind of person that you'd notice anyhow. She dresses in a gray sweatshirt and pants; her face is sullen and pale, her beige hair severely pulled back in a limp ponytail. She's only a teenager, but she seems older, like someone who has already had a disappointing life. The only time Henny cracks a smile is when the colonel gallantly addresses her as Miss Beauregard and insists on carrying her cleaning bucket to and from his room. But then, the colonel is that way with all the girls in the world, defending their honor and stuff.

Lately, Essie keeps crossing paths with Henny, and as part of her sleuthing, Essie jots down whatever the young woman is doing.

This afternoon, she happens into the kitchen as Henny is preparing the colonel's tea tray. The young woman jumps like she has seen a ghost. She tosses an empty tea box hastily in the trash. "What are you doing?" she asks sharply.

What a grouch! But Papa has pointed out that Henny used to have the job of cleaning the whole house. Now that the Swords have agreed to do the cleaning in partial payment of their rent, Henny might resent them. However, Papa, who is nothing if not fair, has also noted that the generous colonel is still paying Henny her full salary for half the work she used to do. "She should actually be glad we've come."

Tell that to Henny, who is flashing Essie the evil eye. Essie stands her ground and stares back. But what she notices is not the expected anger and resentment. Instead, the expression on the young woman's face is closer to loneliness and fear, an orphan look that touches a part of Essie she can't usually get to inside herself.

"I'm sorry," Essie finds herself saying to the young woman. "I didn't mean to scare you. It's just that I'm on the lookout." And then Essie goes on to blab the whole truth without a single white lie. A startled look comes on the teenager's face, like she has been caught with her hand in a cookie jar. Could it be that it was Henny who stole the chips from the bowl left out on the kitchen counter the other night?

"Well, thanks for letting me know," Henny says in a low, conspiring voice. "I'll keep my eyes open and report back to you if I see anything suspicious, all right?"

Essie nods and puts her little notebook away. It's already dawning on her that neither Tía Lola nor Miguel will approve of her confiding in Henny. But what harm can there be in enlisting a fourth pair of watchful eyes— actually, a fifth pair counting Valentino's? Miguel and Tía Lola should be glad for this extra help. Nevertheless, Essie decides not to tell them about Henny. Everywhere people cook beans, Tía Lola likes to say. But people everywhere probably hate blabbermouths who spill them.

●●●

The weekend before Halloween, Linda has to attend an out-of-town conference. It just so happens that on Saturday, Víctor is coaching an away game close by. They decide to meet up and come back together on Sunday. Will Tía Lola mind taking care of both families, preferably in town so she can also keep an eye on the colonel?

"¡No hay problema!" Tía Lola grins happily. No problem. This is precisely the kind of "job" she most enjoys: spending time with the kids and the colonel.

Since he won't be around, Víctor insists on closing the B&B for the weekend. Tía Lola will have enough to do without having to take care of guests, too.

"But the children help me," Tía Lola explains. Still, Mami is worried. What if there is a problem? What if a guest has an accident or the colonel gets sick?

"Hey, I have an idea!" Juanita pipes up. "Us kids can be the guests instead." It'll be like when she ran away from home. "Can we, Tía Lola?"

"*¡No hay problema!*" Tía Lola assures her.

" '*No hay problema*' must be like your mantra, Tía Lola," Essie jokes. She jots down the phrase in her spy book. It might come in useful, should she ever find herself doing detective work in South America.

●●●

Friday morning, while the children are at school, the phone rings. Colonel Charlebois is dozing, so Tía Lola answers the call.

"This is Margaret Soucy," the caller says. The way the woman pronounces her name, it's like she's someone famous whom Tía Lola should know.

"*Buenos días, Señora Soucy.*" Sometimes Tía Lola forgets she is in Vermont and answers automatically in Spanish.

"*Buenos días* to you as well!" The caller is delighted. She is American, but she has lived all over the world, including South America. She rattles on in Spanish with only the trace of an accent.

"I need an out-of-the-way place to stay for a few nights," Margaret goes on to explain. Tía Lola is about to answer that her B&B is closed this weekend, but Margaret adds that hers is a last-minute trip due to a family crisis. *A family crisis.* Those are just the words that touch Tía Lola's heart. Someone is in trouble and needs her help. How can she say no? "We are closed, but if it is just you, we will make an exception," Tía Lola says.

"I'd be much obliged," Margaret says. "You need not

fuss over me. I'm quite self-reliant. I've dipped my gourd in the river with the Jivaros in Peru and hunted with the Bushmen in the Kalahari Desert. Only one other thing: I'd be grateful if you kept my visit under wraps."

"Under what?" Tía Lola asks. Margaret has reverted to English.

"Un secreto," Margaret explains more simply, though her request for secrecy only heightens the mystery.

"No hay problema," Tía Lola agrees, but without her usual perky confidence. Who exactly is this Margaret Soucy? And why does she need a hotel room when she has family in the area? If Tía Lola were keeping a notebook like Essie, she would jot down every one of these interesting details.

●●●

Friday afternoon, as Essie gets off the school bus and heads toward the house, Henny pokes her head out from behind a bush and motions to her. Essie reaches into her pocket for her little notebook. "Put that away," Henny commands. "I need for you to do me a favor," she says more nicely. "There's a guest coming tonight—"

Essie shakes her head. The B&B is closed this weekend. But Henny is certain. "She's arriving late tonight. When she comes, give her this." She offers Essie a folded-up note. "Don't say anything to your aunt about it, okay?"

Essie is feeling increasingly uneasy about all the secrets she is having to keep. It's one thing to tell white lies in her own detective line of work. Another thing to be spraying white lies wherever she goes, till the world is snowed

86

under by untruths. "Why can't you give it to her your-self?"

"Please," the young woman pleads. "I have to get home or my mother'll kill me. I'm already late. I need for you to help me, please."

If Tía Lola's weakness is helping families in trouble, Essie's would have to be rescuing people who are about to be murdered. "Okay," she agrees, taking the note and stuffing it into her pocket.

"And you promise not to tell your aunt?" Henny's eyes cling to Essie with the look of someone who is going to jump off a cliff unless Essie says yes.

Reluctantly, Essie agrees. But she's not happy about being pushed into a corner. As she heads into the house through the back door, Essie notices a piece of litter that must have fallen out of the trash can. It's the flattened box she recalls Henny tossing hurriedly in the trash a few days back. Maybe that's why Essie even bothers to read the name. KNOCK-ME-OUT TEA, the label says.

So intent is Essie on checking out Henny's story that she hurries off without even bothering to jot down this extremely interesting detail in her notebook.

Inside, Tía Lola is indeed telling the assembled group that a guest is coming. "I know we are officially closed, but this is a special situation. And one more thing, our guest wants to be kept a secret."

"Why?" Cari asks, wide-eyed. Secrets can be scary un-less they're about birthday parties.

Tía Lola flashes the little girl a reassuring smile. Maybe

Essie is imagining this, but for a split second, Tía Lola looks worried herself. "Our guest wants privacy. I think she might be famous. Do any of you know a Margaret Soucy?"

The colonel, who is just now rousing himself from his nap, sits up. "Margaret Soucy? Of course, I know Margaret."

No wonder the woman spoke her name as if Tía Lola should know who she is. She's a friend of Colonel Charlebois's. "She has some sort of private family crisis."

"No surprise." The colonel shakes his head sadly. "But it's not so private. The whole town knows about it."

Of course, except for the colonel, all those present are recent newcomers to Bridgeport. None of them has heard the story the old man is about to tell them.

"Margaret Soucy, first of all, is one of *the* best anthropologists of our time. She has lived everywhere and is an authority on any number of curious customs, from child brides in Yemen to cannibalism among the Korowai in New Guinea to snake charmers in Madagascar."

Essie is amazed. She is wasting her time in detective work. And to think this world-famous authority, who has been to even more interesting places than the colonel, is coming to stay in this very house. But why would a blah teenager like Henny be writing to a dazzling world authority who has done the most amazing things?

"Margaret Soucy left town when she was a young girl, not much older than you." The colonel nods at Victoria. "Bright as a whistle. Scholarships at Smith, Stanford. But her sister took the opposite route. She stayed in town, took up with a young fellow who gambled away every last penny she had, then left her with a baby to fend for herself. Unfortunately, this sad turn of events transformed this sister into—sorry to say this about any lady—a bitter, disturbed woman. She and Margaret had a horrible falling-out about, oh, about any number of things." He waves the whole sad affair away and yawns heartily.

He sure is sleepy, Essie finds herself thinking . . . And then, because she just saw the empty box with the interesting name, something finally clicks in Essie's head. Colonel Charlebois has been drinking Knock-Me-Out Tea all day from the thermos Henny prepares for him. No wonder he's dozing off all the time. But why would Henny want to knock out the colonel?

"I am so glad you made an exception in this case," Colonel Charlebois is telling Tía Lola. "Maybe we can be of help in mending the rift in the family. So sad to have a falling-out over that sorry old house. Or the raising of that child, who's now pretty much grown up."

Tía Lola, meanwhile, has been scratching her head over that last name. She has been here now over a year and a half, and she can't recall ever meeting a Soucy. But then, her English is not that good, and sometimes she's not quite sure what she has heard. "Soucy, Soucy," she mulls over the name.

"Soucy is the maiden name. Margaret never got married. Running around the face of creation, how could she?" The colonel sighs, perhaps thinking about his own life. "But her sister, Odette, married a Beauregard. As a matter of fact, the very child in question is Henriette, whom you know as my cleaning girl, Henny. Another reason I kept her on. It's no secret her mother has had many difficulties, and she has the temper to show for it. She might not kill the young lady, but she could certainly make her life miserable."

Essie can't help noticing the startled look on Tía Lola's face. *Aquí hay problema,* her expression seems to be saying. There is a problem here.

Essie herself is feeling so torn. She wants to share the note in her pocket with her fellow detectives. But she promised Henny. Still, Essie knows it is okay to break a promise when keeping a secret might endanger some-body's well-being. But Henny said her mother would kill her. What if something should happen to Henny because Essie betrayed her? Essie would feel terrible. But she re-members a little loophole: Essie promised not to tell her aunt, but she didn't say anything about not telling Miguel.

So after the gathering breaks up, Essie follows Miguel to the baseball bedroom, where he is staying this weekend. "I've got to talk to you," she begins. And then Essie spills the full contents of her overloaded mind to Miguel: how she caught Henny making tea for the colonel and sneakily throwing away the telltale box; how Essie found out what kind of tea was in that box (Knock-Me-Out Tea, get it?); the colonel's always being sleepy these days. Then Essie goes on to relate the encounter with Henny this after-noon in the yard, how the young woman begged her to deliver this secret note to their guest tonight. Essie's hand is shaking so bad, she is glad to hand the note over to Miguel to read out loud:

90

Dear Aunt Margaret,

Things have gotten even more horrible than when I last wrote you. Momma is making me do things I don't think are right. I don't dare write too much. Please meet me tomorrow morning at seven sharp in the backyard of Colonel Charlebois's house. Momma won't suspect anything, as I usually take off then to go clean there. Thank you so much for coming to the rescue. But please don't let anyone see you, as Momma might suspect why you've come.

Your eternally grateful niece,
Henriette

"Wow," Miguel says when he finishes reading.

"You said it." Essie is feeling relieved that she has a friend like Miguel to confide in. "Should we tell Tía Lola, you think?"

Miguel looks up at the ceiling as if the answer were written there. Then he takes a deep breath before shaking his head. "I think we should solve this mystery ourselves. Because if we tell, you know what is going to happen?"

"What?"

"Mami and your father will worry that a B&B is too dangerous. Tía Lola will feel that she made a big mistake exposing us and the colonel to this danger. Tía Lola's B&B will close forever. We will all go back to our boring lives."

Boring lives. The words fall like heavy stones to the bottom of Essie's heart. The cold is setting in. The dead of winter is coming. Month upon month of being cooped up doing homework, uninteresting chores. Miguel is right. Better to solve the mystery themselves than to end up in a boring life.

"So, what do you say?" Miguel is looking Essie straight in the eye, as if daring her to prove she's not a baby who believes in ghosts.

Essie would not turn down a dare if her life depended on it, which she sincerely hopes doesn't. *"No hay problema,"* she bluffs in her best imitation of a brave detective in South America.

chapter eight

How the Mystery of the B&B Mishaps Was Solved

As the two children shake on solving the B&B mystery all by themselves, Miguel can't help noticing that Essie's hand is ice cold. He half hopes that she will back down and insist they tell Tía Lola. What if they are in way over their heads and something scary happens?

It doesn't help that it's almost Halloween—that spooky time of year. As they await Margaret Soucy's arrival this windy Friday night, the two children jump at the creepy sounds the old house is making. Miguel glances at the maple tree out the window, and his heart stops. The bare branches look like gnarled fingers reaching in to grab him.

It's way after supper when they hear the front-door knocker. Miguel and Essie exchange a long, hopeless look. Miguel's stomach is doing flip-flops. But every time he feels himself slipping into doubts, he repeats the word

"Booooooooring," drawing it out to make it even more unappealing. Anything to avoid the B&B closing.

At the bottom of the stairs, the two children join Tía Lola and Colonel Charlebois, who are coming into the mudroom from the parlor. It's like there's a welcome committee at this B&B.

"Bienvenida," Tía Lola says, throwing open the door. But the spookiest thing, there's no one out there to receive her welcome. Only leaves blowing about in the howling wind.

"Well, I'll be!" Colonel Charlebois exclaims. "I could have sworn—"

Just then, *wham!* Out from the darkness leaps a gorilla. They all cry out, even the colonel, although almost immediately, he steps forward to protect the ladies. If only Essie had brought her samurai sword along. But the very next moment, Miguel is glad she didn't. Off comes the gorilla mask, and there's a tall, big-boned woman laughing in front of them.

"Margaret Soucy," the colonel scolds. "You should be ashamed of yourself!"

"Just a harmless seasonal joke." The woman is still laughing, a hee-haw laugh that makes Miguel think of a donkey. "But I had no idea when I called that this would be your B&B, Uncle Charlie." *Uncle* Charlie?! Colonel Charlebois didn't say anything about being related to Margaret Soucy.

"First off, there's nothing harmless about giving an old man a heart attack. And second of all, this isn't my B&B, but Tía Lola's here, along with her friends."

Poor Tía Lola still has her hand on her heart, trying to calm herself after her fright. *"Bienvenida,"* she manages again, but this welcome is a lot less bouncy than her first one.

"Pleased to make your acquaintance." Margaret Soucy pumps each of their hands so forcefully, Miguel can feel his whole body shaking. When she gets to Colonel Charlebois, she throws her arms around him. In her big, puffy parka, she could be mistaken for a gorilla from the back, dressed up as a human being.

Despite his initial scare, the colonel seems truly delighted to see her. It's not every day that a famous native daughter returns for a visit. "What's it been, over ten years?"

"Good question." Margaret Soucy looks off as if the answer were a wildebeest grazing in the distance. Was it before her MacArthur genius grant or after her book on child brides? "Oh, whatever." She dismisses these achievements with a wave of her hand. "I'm just so glad to see you, Uncle Charlie. I was sure by now you'd be six feet under." What a thing to say to the old man!

Essie has been searching for a resemblance between their tall, boisterous guest and the stooped old man. Nothing matches up. "So, are you guys really related?"

"Only in temperament," Margaret Soucy says, heehawing all over again. When she laughs, her upper lip peels back, exposing her prominent teeth. It must take her twice the amount of time of a normal person to brush them.

After a cup of ginger tea, Miguel and Essie escort their guest upstairs to her tropical bedroom. "I'll be right at home!" she exclaims, and launches into one of her amazing

Amazonian adventures. This woman has not known a boring moment in her adult life, Miguel can see that. It's a full twenty minutes before there's a break for Miguel to hand over the note from Henny.

"And what's this?" Margaret Soucy asks, intrigued. For a moment, Miguel can see the curiosity that has made this woman a successful anthropologist. It's as if he has handed over a bone from the first human being. "Mmm," she keeps saying, as if savoring the contents of the note. Recalling how the colonel mentioned that Margaret Soucy once lived among cannibals, Miguel wonders if Margaret Soucy has ever eaten a human being herself. Maybe when he gets to know her better, he can ask her.

When Margaret finally looks up, she seems surprised to find Miguel and Essie still standing before her. "I think it's time to say *oyasumi, allin tuta,* and *gudnaet*—that's Japanese, Quechuan, and Solomon Island pidgin for 'good night.' May you live to see the morning light," she adds eerily. The next moment, she's laughing her toothy hee-haw laughter again. "That's how the Itabo say good night. By the way, either of you youngsters interested in a used gorilla mask?"

Of course, Essie snatches it up. As the two children exit the room, Margaret Soucy calls after them, "You children sleep tight." And then Miguel could swear he hears her add, "Don't let the cannibals bite!"

●●●

Miguel spends the night running away from cannibals in his dreams. Next thing he knows, Essie is shaking him awake. Last night before turning in, they agreed to meet downstairs in the backyard by a quarter to seven. Just in time to hide and spy on the secret meeting between aunt and niece.

"Come on, Miguel! I already hear her in the bathroom."

Thank goodness Miguel slept in his clothes as a precaution. In no time, the two children are bounding downstairs and through the kitchen on their way to the backyard. One thing they should have anticipated: Tía Lola is already awake, standing by the stove, frying up some bacon. *"Buenos días. ¡Qué sorpresa!"* What a surprise to see the kids up this early on a Saturday morning!

"Um . . . uh . . . um," Essie begins. It's as if she just learned a tribal language from Margaret Soucy, full of grunts and onomatopoetic sounds.

Esperanza Espada at a loss for words? You bet this makes Tía Lola suspicious. "Okay. *¿Qué pasa?*" What's up?

At last, Essie finds her tongue. "We're just going out to get some exercise before breakfast, Tía Lola." For proof, she whacks the air with her samurai sword, which she thought to bring along this time, just in case.

Tía Lola cocks her head, unconvinced. But she is soon distracted by the sound of their guest coming down the stairs, calling out good morning in several languages. The children slip out the back door and head for the woodpile. They crouch down just in time, as here comes Henny, rounding the side of the house, looking over her shoulder. The back door opens again, and Margaret Soucy steps out.

It takes a moment for the long-absent aunt to recognize

her grown-up niece. "Henriette! Is that you?" she calls out. Henny swivels around and runs toward her aunt, looking like a shipwreck victim who has finally sighted land. She collapses, sobbing, in Margaret's arms.

"There, there." Margaret keeps patting her niece's back as if she were burping a baby. After a while, Henny calms down and leads her aunt to a bench in the back of the yard. "Let's talk here. Any other place in town, well, I'm just afraid it might get back to Momma."

At the mention of her sister, Margaret Soucy's face tightens. "How is Odette?"

The question unstoppers Henny's bottled-up feelings. Before they've even sat down, Henny is pouring her heart out to her aunt. How her mother got so furious about the competition from Tía Lola's B&B. How she was especially upset about this "foreign woman" putting her out of business.

"Odette did that on her very own," Margaret Soucy remarks. "Her bad character would put the Ritz out of business."

But what sent Henny's mother over the top was when another foreign-sounding family, the Espadas, moved in with the colonel, and her own daughter was demoted to part-time cleaning. "She just flipped! Even though I told her Colonel Charlebois was still paying me my full salary. She didn't care. She wanted revenge . . . And she made me . . . oh, Aunt Margaret, I was just so scared."

"Made you do what, child?"

Henny bursts into sobs again. The story comes out in bits and pieces. How Henny smeared Vaseline all over the water polo team's equipment. How she steamed open an envelope and changed the address on the groom's family's wedding invitation.

Miguel and Essie exchange a look of amazement. So Henny and her mother are the culprits! Essie's grip tightens on her sword. In case Henny gets out of hand.

"And yesterday, Momma somehow found out that a guest was coming here. No, she doesn't know it's you, Aunt Margaret. She ordered me to go in the guest room and put these in your bed." Henny pulls out a bag of plastic critters: spiders, squiggly worms, and long, rubbery snakes.

Margaret Soucy's mouth twists scornfully. "I hate to tell sis, but these would not have scared me in the least. Why, I've slept in the jungle with crocodiles and scorpions and poisonous snakes. I've eaten beetles and tarantulas and three kinds of locusts."

Miguel and Essie are glad they have not yet had breakfast, otherwise it might come back to haunt them now. Just when they're on the brink of solving the mystery of the B&B mishaps, they don't need another mishap.

"But the worst part, the part I'm most ashamed of—on account of Colonel Charlebois is, like, the nicest person to me in the world—is what I've been doing to him." Henny pauses, as if she herself can't believe what she has done. "Momma made me fill his thermos with Knock-Me-Out Tea."

"Knock out Uncle Charlie? My sister is trying to kill our old family friend?" Even Margaret Soucy, who has lived among cannibals, is shocked.

"No, no, not kill," Henny explains. "Just put him to sleep so I can sneak in when everyone else goes out and do all the tricks I told you about that'll make the B&B have to close down."

Margaret Soucy looks like she just got pierced with a poisoned spear. "You should have come to me sooner, Henriette," she says. All her silly feuding with her sister has fallen by the wayside. "And I'm sorry, but I'm going to have to talk to the police. Your mother needs help." Then after a pause, in an even sadder voice, she adds, "You need help."

This news, of course, sets off another round of Henny's tears. "Oh please, Aunt Margaret, I don't want to go to jail. I don't want Momma to go to jail. I'll make it up to the colonel. I'll clean his house for the rest of my life, for nothing."

"We'll have to see," Margaret Soucy says. She has studied human beings on every continent, and one thing she has learned: in order to ensure justice on this planet, young and old have to be held responsible for their actions. But justice without forgiveness won't make the world a better place. "People do have to take responsibility for their actions, Henriette. But maybe if your mother confesses, we can get you both into a diversion program."

"Momma will never confess," Henny says bleakly. "You know her, Aunt Margaret."

"But what if we have proof? I don't mean your word against hers. I mean hard evidence. What if we caught her in the act?"

"But how?" Henny throws up her hands. "She always has me do stuff for her."

For the first time since Miguel laid eyes on her, Margaret Soucy looks totally stumped. She might know how to eat tarantulas and sleep with cobras and protect herself against cannibals, but she doesn't know how to catch her own sister red-handed.

They have all been so intent on Henny's confession that they've missed the figure who slipped out the back door a while ago, wondering where her guest was going and why the children had been exercising so long. When Tía Lola finally speaks up, everyone jumps. Miguel and Essie are flushed out of their hiding place. "I have an idea for how to catch your mother, Henrieta. And I am sure if you cooperate with us, it will go easier for you."

Henny is already nodding, without yet knowing what Tía Lola is going to suggest.

Before she unveils her plan, Tía Lola turns to Miguel and Essie. "I am disappointed you didn't tell me the truth. You know Tía Lola would always try to help you."

"It's my fault, Tía Lola," Miguel confesses. Like Margaret Soucy said, people have to take responsibility for their actions. And it was his idea to keep the mystery solving a secret. "We were afraid you might decide to close down your B&B."

"Close it down?" Tía Lola is shaking her head with her whole body. "And what? Give Odette Beauregard exactly what she wants? *¡No, señor!* I know what will make her come around so we can catch her in the act."

"You do?" It's as close to a chorus as any four people not in a chorus can be.

"It's called the Messenger Hasn't Come Back strategy," Tía Lola says. Seeing their baffled looks, she goes on to explain: "Henrieta's mother has sent her on a mission. What if Henrieta doesn't come back? Her mother will eventually come to find out what happened to her messenger."

"Ingenious! Worthy of the wise Kogis." This is Margaret Soucy, world authority, commending Tía Lola, who never went past fourth grade. "But will it work?"

Tía Lola nods with certainty. "Believe me. One thing I know from living in your United States of American tribe, Margarita, is that curiosity killed the cat." Tía Lola grins, pleased at the opportunity to use a saying she recently learned in English.

Miguel sure hopes Tía Lola's plan will work. She has a good track record. After all, it was her Thin Edge of the Wedge idea that got the B&B ball rolling with the guinea-pig weekend. Unless the offender is caught and safely put where she can't cause any more harm, Miguel is sure that Mami and Víctor will close down Tía Lola's B&B—even if his aunt would rather keep it open to spite Mrs. Beauregard.

"In order for this plan to work, you must stay out of sight inside the house," Tía Lola cautions Henny. "Your mother will come around, but it might take a while."

"When she does, she'll kill me." Henny has started worrying again.

But her bold, brave aunt throws an arm around her niece and gives her a hearty shake. "Courage, my dear.

One thing I learned from the Bushmen in the Kalahari, when you hunt the kudu, it's persistence that wins out."

Soon they are launched into another one of Margaret Soucy's incredible adventures. Miguel can't help thinking that if a Bushman with a bow and arrow can bring down a large animal, surely five people, one of them armed with a samurai sword, can handle Henny's crazy mother.

❋❋❋

But by late afternoon, Miguel is not so sure Tía Lola's plan is going to work. They've been waiting all day, and still no sign of Mrs. Beauregard. Every hour or so, he and Essie make the rounds, inspecting the yard for fresh footprints. Finally, Miguel and Essie decide to go check why Mrs. Beauregard hasn't come in search of her messenger.

The two children ride their bikes out to Miguel's house in the country. Miguel has hatched his own plan: baiting Henny's mother with her very own bag of fake critters.

As they ride by Mrs. Beauregard's house, they spot a figure behind the thin curtain in the front parlor. Past the house, they turn around. As they pedal by again, Miguel hurls one of the spiders against the window. The fake tarantula lands with a thud. Good thing his pitching arm is still strong, even if he's months out of training.

As the two children ride away, the front door opens. Mrs. Beauregard comes out to investigate. She must have found the spider, because she calls out tentatively, "Henny?" Then in a louder, more threatening voice, she says, "Henriette Beauregard, you are in a heap of trouble!"

By this time, Miguel and Essie have reached the corner. They stop and hide behind a bush to watch.

Down the road comes Mrs. Beauregard, her slippers slapping on the pavement, her coat unbuttoned, her loose hair blowing about wildly. Just past the house, she finds one of the snakes Miguel dropped. A few steps later, a beetle. Miguel's plan is working! He'll keep dropping them all the way to Tía Lola's B&B. A kind of reverse Hansel and Gretel, in which the children lure the witch out of her den and into the hands of the sheriff.

Miguel and Essie get back on their bikes, ready to ride ahead of their prey. But just then, Mrs. Beauregard stumbles. The light is dim. She must not have seen a pothole or a rock and has taken what looks to be a nasty fall.

"Let's go for help," Essie urges Miguel. Soon it'll be dark. They should not be on an unlit country road without reflective jackets on.

Miguel would like to ride safely back as well. But he's not about to desert a wounded person, even if she happens to be someone who has done mean things and deserves her comeuppance. "You go. Tell Tía Lola to call an ambulance. I'll stay with her."

"S-s-s-stay alone with Mrs. B-B-B-Beauregard?" Essie's voice is all trembly.

So as not to betray his own shaky voice, Miguel nods. He turns his bike around and rides back to the crumpled heap on the side of the road. There's a pool of blood beside her head. Miguel springs from his bike and kneels down at her side. "Are you all right?"

In response, Mrs. Beauregard groans. Never has Miguel

been so glad to hear a human sound. "Just lie there, don't try to move. My friend's gone for help."

"No, no, don't," the woman cries, struggling to get up. But with a yelp of pain, she lets herself fall back onto the road. Miguel pulls off his jacket and lays it under her head. In the faint light of the setting sun, he can see that her right foot is twisted. Blood is coming from the cut on her forehead. Everything else seems to be okay. But one thing Miguel learned in their first-aid class at school is not to move someone who has been in an accident. You can make things worse. Dislocate a broken back. Cause more bleeding. All this he relates to Mrs. Beauregard in a calm voice.

"It's going to be okay," he keeps telling her.

A surprised look has come over Mrs. Beauregard's face. It's as if for the first time in a long while, she is realizing that somebody does care for her. This boy stopped to help. He took off his jacket to make her comfortable. Maybe the world isn't a totally miserable place. Maybe there are these moments of amazing grace. "You're a kind young man," she murmurs. "Thank you, son."

● ● ●

Sunday afternoon, Víctor and Mami return to a quiet, peaceful gathering in the front parlor. Tía Lola and the colonel sit in their rocking chairs, accompanied by two strangers, one of them in a cast. The Espada girls and Juanita and Miguel are finishing up their homework. Linda and Víctor look at each other with lifted eyebrows. Kids doing their homework without their parents reminding them!

Tía Lola and the colonel have agreed to tell Linda and Víctor the news in small portions. Otherwise, they might be tempted to close down Tía Lola's B&B, especially if they are given a full serving of this weekend's misadventures.

And now, more than ever, a new hotel will be needed in town, as Mrs. Beauregard's place will be closing down. All day the two sisters have been talking. Odette has confessed her wrongdoing and begged forgiveness. Meanwhile, Margaret has taken responsibility for her own pigheadedness, leaving her sister and young niece to fend for themselves. The sheriff has already been by, and though no one is pressing charges, Mrs. Beauregard and Henny have agreed to enroll in a diversion program and get some counseling.

What turned their lives around? For Henny, it was Essie's confiding in her. "Here this little kid was trusting me, and I was being a sneak. I felt this big," she says, pinching the air with her thumb and forefinger.

For her mother, what melted her cold heart was Miguel's kindness. "This boy, who didn't owe me a darn thing, took care of me. I'll never forget it." Mrs. Beauregard's eyes fill with tears.

Miguel comes clean. It was his baiting Mrs. Beauregard with those plastic critters that caused the problem in the first place. "I'm sorry you got hurt."

But Mrs. Beauregard won't have it. That fall has led to her lifting herself up out of the pit she had fallen into. "Amazing grace, like the song says. You did a kind, thoughtful deed by stopping." Actually, when Mrs. Beauregard fell, Miguel didn't even have to think about it. Of course he ran back to help her. It's what you should do as a member of the human-being tribe. Margaret Soucy can tell you that.

But the biggest surprise of the weekend so far is that Margaret Soucy has decided to come home. She is tired of traveling, all those airplane flights, elephant rides, trekking through deserts and jungles. All those bad meals of spiders and locusts and yak's milk. She's ready to hang up her binoculars and netted hat. To settle down with her sister and niece and guide them both into happier, healthier lives.

Víctor surveys the cozy scene. "How lovely to find everyone safe and sound and happy." His eyes land on the Soucy sisters. "I believe we haven't met."

"These are some nieces of mine," Colonel Charlebois speaks up. It's the truth. Since childhood, the two Soucy girls, who lived down the road from his family farm, have called him Uncle Charlie. They might as well be relatives.

Once the introductions are over, Linda and Víctor exchange a long glance. It seems they, too, have some news to share. But first, Mami asks, "So how was your weekend?"

No one says a word. They all stare at the floor, afraid to catch each other's eye and explode with laughter. Thank goodness for Margaret Soucy, who never met a silence she couldn't fill with stories of her adventures.

"I was actually telling the children about my time among the Itabo."

"She was indeed," Colonel Charlebois asserts. "Fascinating stories."

107

"And I was telling about my childhood in the *campo*." Tía Lola is not one to be left behind when it comes to stories. This is another of her ploys, along with The Thin Edge of the Wedge and The Messenger Hasn't Come Back. It's called the Arabian Nights strategy. You find yourself in a tight spot and you start telling stories to save your life. One story sparks another and another. By the time 1,001 stories have been told, no one remembers to cut off anybody's head or close down anybody's B&B.

Víctor and Linda listen delightedly to Margaret and Tía Lola. Then, in a quiet lull between stories, Cari asks the question that stops all the storytellers in their tracks. "What I want to know is: are we going to keep having Tía Lola's B&B or not?"

Everyone turns to Tía Lola. *"Vamos a ver,"* she says mysteriously, winking at the colonel. We shall see.

chapter nine

How Cari Got Her Answer
and a BIG New *Familia* Was Formed

Remember that look that passed between Linda and Víctor? During the weekend away, the two parents have had a chance to talk.

Víctor has finally confessed that he doesn't want to be a lawyer anymore. And it's for the best. His part-time coaching job at the college will officially become full-time, starting in January! How happy he is with this opportunity to follow his dreams.

That's not the only dream that has come true. Víctor has proposed, and Linda has said yes!

But now they need Tía Lola's help. What is the best way to tell the children that they would like to get married and form a big family together?

As Tía Lola is mulling this over, she gets a call from Daniel and Carmen in Brooklyn. They have been debating where and when to get married. Ever since she slept in the bridal bedroom, Carmen has been dreaming of staying at Tía Lola's B&B for her honeymoon. They'd like to come up this weekend and discuss options and possibly work out the details.

And so Tía Lola plans the biggest, most ambitious weekend at her B&B so far, with all the families coming together under one roof. Carmen and Daniel and Linda will each get a guest bedroom; Víctor, the kids, and Tía Lola will stay up in the attic. This will be a trial run of the big new *familia* that the children and adults will all be forming together.

"Perhaps I'll go stay out of the way in the farmhouse," the colonel offers.

Tía Lola won't hear of it. "You can't leave, *coronel*! You have to stay and help me. After all, you and I are the fairy godparents."

"Well, I don't know about that," the colonel says crankily. He's not the fairy-godfather type. He has been too many years in the military. But the last year of getting close to Miguel and Juanita's family has softened the old man's crusty character, and the arrival of the Espadas has further sweetened his temperament. "Just as long as I don't have to go around carrying a wand and wearing wings instead of my uniform, I guess I can join in."

No wand, no wings, Tía Lola promises, saluting him.

❋❋❋

The night before all the parents are due to arrive, Tía Lola and Colonel Charlebois hold a meeting with Miguel and Juanita and the Espada sisters. None of the children know the specifics of why all the parents are gathering. But hey, kids are smart. They've figured out what is coming down the pike.

"Big surprise: our parents are getting hooked up." Essie sighs one of those been-there-done-that sighs.

Tía Lola's hands are at her hips. "Esperanza Espada, there's more to family than 'hooking up,' as you call it. Isn't that so, *coronel*?"

"How would I know?" Colonel Charlebois replies gruffly. The military has been his only family all his adult life. "But yes, yes, of course, I imagine that is so." He did agree to be a fairy godfather. This means being an authority on any number of things.

"It's extremely important that each of you takes part in your parents' remarriages," Tía Lola's voice has assumed a serious tone. A somber mood settles in the room.

"But I don't get it, Tía Lola." Juanita speaks up for all of them. "What are we supposed to do? We're not the ones getting married."

"Oh no?!" Tía Lola raises her eyebrows at the colonel as if she can't believe these kids have gotten this far in life without knowing what's what. "Your parents are not just marrying their new spouses, they are marrying your new stepparents. Anything you'd love to see in your new family or anything you want to keep from the old, now is the time to say so."

111

It's nice of Tía Lola to look out for their interests. But the children aren't really worried. Never mind the bad rap that fairy tales have given stepmothers, especially. Every one of their soon-to-be stepparents is a really nice person.

"You *are* very lucky children," Tía Lola is saying, as if reading their minds. But she has her own reason for saying so. "In this country, children have only nuclear families: mama, papa. That's it!" She holds out two empty palms. "So few to love and be loved by. Back home, we have huge *familias,* with *mamá, papá, abuelitos,* grandparents, *tíos, tías,* uncles and aunts, *primos, primas,* cousins and more cousins, and many *amigos.* Now you, too, will have a big *familia* in *this* country." Tía Lola starts counting them off: Linda, Víctor, Daniel, Carmen, Abuelito, Abuelita, *el coronel.* . . .

"But wait, Tía Lola," Essie stops her. "Daniel and Carmen aren't related to us." She points to her sisters and herself.

"*¿Qué no?* Oh no? Of course they will be. Daniel is the father and Carmen will become the stepmother of your stepsisters. So they are your stepparents once removed!"

Essie can buy that. After all, the Espada girls have been calling Tía Carmen aunt for as long as they can remember. Carmen and Papa used to work together in the same law firm in New York. In fact, if Carmen hadn't recommended Víctor for Tía Lola's immigration hearing, this story wouldn't be happening at all.

"Sometime this weekend, we will have a big meeting of the whole *familia.*" Tía Lola spreads her arms as if she means to hug all of them. "Each of you will get your chance to tell your wishes."

"Is there a limit?" Essie *would* ask.

"Because you are many, why don't you each pick one thing that you'd like to see in the new family, and one thing you'd like to keep from the old one?"

For the rest of the evening at Tía Lola's B&B, the children are quiet, thinking over their memories, their hopes, and their dreams. Even Valentino stares pensively into the fire, wondering how best to convey his own doggy desires.

❋❋❋

Saturday night, after all the guests have had a day to settle in, Tía Lola calls for a gathering in the front parlor. "*Todos.* Everyone. Including our one-and-only *mascota,*" she adds. Valentino loves the Spanish word for "pet." It makes him feel that he's not just a pet, but the mascot of the family.

Tía Lola explains why she is holding this meeting. How they will soon all be one *familia.* How everyone in a *familia* gets a vote, just like in this great United States of America, with people coming from around the world to form one country together. "You, grown-ups, have had a chance to share your hopes and fears with each other. Now the children would like their turn."

Tía Lola glances over at the children, sitting together for moral support. "Who would like to start?"

No surprise, Essie does. "We all agreed on the one thing we'd like to keep, Papa." Suddenly, very uncharacteristically, Essie is stricken with speechlessness. She turns to her big sister. "You say it."

"Thanks a lot," Victoria mutters under her breath.

Essie *would* pull a "You're the oldest" when faced with something she doesn't want to do. "First, let's each say what we want in our new family, okay?" she suggests, delaying the uncomfortable request.

This part is no problem for Essie. "I'd like for our whole new family—you guys, too . . ." She nods toward Daniel and Carmen. Before Papa can stop her with that look of his, Essie races through her wish: "I'd like us to all gotoDisneyWorldlikeyoupromised, Papa." Earlier this year, Papa said he would consider a trip to Disney World. Instead, he brought his daughters to Vermont, which Essie has to admit turned out to be fun. But still. Essie can't help feeling shortchanged.

Incredibly, Papa says, "Well, Essie, you're in luck."

Linda elaborates. "Your father and I have been talking about going to the D.R. so my *familia* there can meet our new family. Disney World is on the way—"

Before she can finish, the room explodes with cheering. Two cool trips in one! Essie especially goes ballistic, as her older sister calls it, high-fiving everybody, including Valentino. Finally she settles down so her little sister can have a turn.

"For something new, I want a little baby sister," Cari whispers. "I promise I'll carry her with both hands." She shows how she will do it.

"We'll definitely work on it," Carmen promises her, biting her lip so as not to smile. "Except it might turn out to be a little boy. Would that be okay?"

"Just as long as it's littler than me," Cari says, relieved that her wish is being taken seriously.

Victoria levels one of her killer looks at Essie. Don't you dare. It would be just like Essie to make fun of Cari by reminding her that a baby sister or brother has to be littler than she. But the look is lost on Essie, who is already far away in Disney World, zooming down Space Mountain, screaming her head off.

Victoria is next. She feels timid about wishing for stuff after her water polo boy-wish fiasco. She settles on something that's not too personal—so she won't feel awful if it backfires on her. "I know this is going to sound weird because we're Mexican-Americans. But, Papa, like you've told us, you were raised almost totally in English. You guys know so much more Spanish." Victoria nods at Miguel and Juanita. "I'd really like it if we spoke Spanish sometimes as a family. Like maybe even pick a day a week?"

Ding-dong goes the homework warning bell in Miguel's head. But Miguel also feels pleased to be complimented on his Spanish. And with Tía Lola in charge, this wish could turn out to be fun. Only problem is his little sister. Having a second language will only increase Juanita's territory for showing off how special she is.

"*No hay problema,* right, Tía Lola?" Juanita says, as if on cue.

Victoria takes a deep breath. Here goes the awkward request. "For our family wish of something we'd like to keep . . ." Victoria hesitates. She doesn't want to hurt anybody's feelings. But with a stepmother about to enter the scene, all three sisters are aching for a way to include their own mother in this new *familia.*

"It's about Mama." Victoria glances toward her father, not sure that she should continue.

"Go ahead, Victoria. It's okay," her father reassures her.

"We want to keep doing something special on Mama's birthday." Then the harder words to say, "Just us." This is a tradition they all came up with when their mother died three years ago. On the first anniversary of her birthday, the family went out to Montauk, a place Mama loved. On the second birthday, the family attended a concert of really pretty music Mama liked to play on the piano. This year they went camping by a waterfall where Mama and Papa had gone on their honeymoon.

Víctor pulls his three teary-eyed girls toward him. "Of course we'll keep having our own special day," he promises them.

"What a beautiful way to remember your mother," Linda says, tearing up herself.

More than anything she could say, these words endear her to Víctor's three daughters. They will not have to choose between their stepmother and their own mother. Víctor sighs, gazing with gratitude at his bride-to-be.

"Our turn," Juanita pipes up, eager to say what she'd like to keep from her old family. She has done the math. There are four big bedrooms on the second floor in the old farmhouse, as well as two little attic bedrooms, one of them being Tía Lola's. There isn't enough room for everyone to have their very own bedroom. "I want to be able to keep my room by myself."

"We'll see about that," her mother says noncommittally.

Juanita presses on as if her mother had said yes. "And

for my new wish"—Juanita steels herself not to look over at Essie—"I want to change the decoration of my room to be like a bride's room."

A shocked Essie comes hurtling back from Space Mountain. Another girly girl in the family! But Essie knows better than to show her disgust by sticking her forefinger into her mouth and risk Papa canceling the trip to Disney World until Essie learns her manners.

"And from my other family—"

"You've had your two wishes already," her brother points out.

"But we've got two new stepparents." Juanita appeals to their aunt. "Right, Tía Lola, that we can have two wishes for each new family?"

Before Tía Lola can deliver a verdict, Carmen pleads Juanita's case. "I'd actually love to hear any suggestions for things to keep from your old family."

"I want to be able to keep coming down any time we want to see Papi," Juanita blurts out the minute Tía Lola nods. And then, without warning, she is crying. The adults all swing into consolation mode. Mami puts her arm around Juanita; Carmen squeezes her free hand; Papi strokes her head. "Of course, of course," they all keep coo-ing like she's a little baby.

If his sister had stuck to the rules, this meltdown could have been avoided. Especially since Miguel's wish is this same exact one, and he could have said it for both of them without bawling.

Juanita gives her nose a final blow. "Your turn, Miguel," she sniffles.

"Ditto on that wish," Miguel says, trying to avoid another scene. "And for my new family, I'd like to have a friend stay over even if it's a weeknight." His *mami* is pretty good about letting him have friends over on weekends. But with so many girls around, Miguel will occasionally need another boy in the house even if it is a weeknight. "It's just a lot of sisters," he adds, as his mother is looking like she might veto his request. But the word "sisters" warms her heart. The thin edge of the wedge, Tía Lola would call it.

"Poor Miguelito," Mami sympathizes.

There's another wish Miguel would make if he thought it would do any good. He doesn't want to be called "little Miguel" anymore. Bad enough that he's losing his place as the eldest. At least he will continue to be the eldest son.

"Maybe we can have a man's night out," Víctor puts in. "Go to Rudy's. Afterward catch a movie. In the summer, throw some pitches."

This sounds awesome! But Miguel doesn't want to seem too excited and hurt his father's feelings. No matter how great a stepfather Víctor will be, he will never ever replace Papi.

"I think these are all cool wishes," his father is saying. Víctor nods. Meanwhile, Linda and Carmen are both dabbing their eyes, touched by the loving spirit among all the families.

As if he were the gavel concluding the meeting, Valentino starts barking. The room explodes with laughter, thinking Valentino is just being his cute doggy-wanting-to-be-a-human-being self. He barks again, more insistently.

Tía Lola intervenes on his behalf. After several months, she has become quite proficient in dog language. "Valentino says he wants his turn. For his new wish for the new family, he would like to cast his vote to move out to the country, where he can run free."

The children again break into cheering. The truth is, if you are going to be in Vermont, it makes sense to live out in the country, surrounded by rolling hills and green pastures. A dog can feel like he doesn't have to die to be in heaven.

Tía Lola cocks her ear and listens to Valentino's little barks and pants to be sure she understands. "As for what Valentino would like from his old family, he votes that we keep Tía Lola's B&B open."

Víctor and Linda are about to say, "We'll have to see about that." For one thing, how can they live in the country and still run a B&B in town? But they are drowned out by the renewed cheering and clapping of five children, two fairy godparents, and the insistent barking of Valentino.

The four parents exchange a worried glance. It's as if they just now did the math and realized they are in deep trouble. Anything that comes up for a vote, they will be outnumbered.

chapter ten

How Tía Lola's Wish Came True

There's no denying there is a contradiction in Valentino's wishes, which Víctor points out once the children have quieted down. They cannot both live in the country and run a B&B in town.

"At least we can grant half of your wish, old boy," Víctor consoles Valentino. The family will move out to the farmhouse as soon as he and Linda marry.

"And I can grant the other half!" Tía Lola offers. Nothing she likes better than to make a wish come true. "When your family moves in, I will leave the country." She announces this so cheerfully, the children can't believe it. This is the worst news in the world! Tía Lola isn't going to stay? This was just a visit after all?

Juanita's wish has backfired on her! She is ready to sleep in the garden shed if that's what it takes to keep Tía

Lola with them. "Please, Tía Lola, I'll share my room, please. Don't go back to the Dominican Republic."

"If you leave, I will, too!" Essie folds her arms and lifts her chin in defiance. Too late, she realizes this is not a smart move. You don't bail out of a family that will soon be going to Disney World.

"*Un momento.*" Tía Lola holds up one hand. Who said anything about leaving the country-country? She meant leaving the country, as in "out in the country," where Miguel and Juanita live. English is so confusing! "I will move into town to run the B&B, if the *coronel* permits. This way he won't be left alone."

"Don't worry about me," the old man says in a gruff voice, but he is touched by Tía Lola's offer. He has grown used to good company. And he so enjoys having a B&B in his house. It brings interesting people to his doorstep now that he is no longer able to travel around the world meeting them.

"For me, as well, *coronel,* it will be a pleasure to start over with a new adventure." This would be Tía Lola's wish come true: her very own place where the whole world can come visit and stay! "And any of you, children, who want to spend the night, the week, the month, in town at Tía Lola's B&B are more than welcome!"

"Sounds to me like the best of both worlds," Papa says, already promoting the idea that a moment ago seemed impossible. "But one thing that still intrigues me," he adds, fixing his gaze on the family *mascota,* "why would Valentino vote for your B&B to continue if he's going to be with us in the country?"

121

Tía Lola shrugs. "You'll have to ask him."

Valentino wags his tail at his master, a dog's way of smiling and evading the question. As much as he loves the country, Valentino is planning on being a frequent visitor at Tía Lola's B&B in town. He has found that guests tend to be quite generous with treats—especially if he does cute stuff like fetch their slippers from upstairs when they are sitting by the fire or bring in the paper while they are eating breakfast. However, it's probably not in his best interests to share this discovery with Víctor. Next thing he knows, there'll be a sign posted in the dining room: PLEASE DO NOT FEED THE DOG.

"It's definitely going to be an exciting year," Carmen exclaims happily. "Two marriages, a move to the country, a permanent B&B in town!"

"Two trips," Essie is quick to add.

"And one huge birthday party," Tía Lola says, turning her bright gaze at the colonel, who scowls back like the sun is in his eyes.

"Don't even think of it!" he tells her. But that is like telling someone, "Do not think of an elephant in the room." That's all anyone can think of: the colonel's eighty-fifth birthday on the ninth of December.

● ● ●

That night, Miguel has a dream. Cannibals are chasing after him again! This time they catch him and carry him off to their village, where Miguel is sure a big pot of boiling water awaits him. Instead, he comes upon the most astonishing surprise: the whole tribe is wearing party hats and blowing whistles and popping favors. Sitting at the center of the circle with everyone singing "Happy Birthday" in Spanish is Tía Lola!

When he wakes up, Miguel lies in bed wondering, When exactly *is* Tía Lola's birthday? Every time he asks, Tía Lola just waves him off.

Miguel corners his mother coming out of her room. But Mami herself doesn't know for sure, just that it's sometime in December.

"When I was growing up, we were so poor that Tía Lola never made a point about her birthday. But she made a big deal about celebrating mine, including always telling me a special story." As to how old Tía Lola is going to be, Mami is not really sure about that either. "It's like her beauty mark, sometimes it's here, sometimes there." Mami points to her right cheek, then to the center of her forehead. "Sometimes Tía Lola is fifty-two, sometimes she's fifty-five." The point is Tía Lola is young at heart, no matter how old she is on the calendar. "But why this sudden curiosity about her exact birthday?"

So Miguel tells his *mami* his dream. That's where he got the idea. "We should give Tía Lola a birthday party this year. You've said yourself, she's never had one."

Mami hesitates. "It's a lovely idea. But you don't know your aunt. She's worse than the colonel, and more mobile. The minute she finds out we're planning a party for her, she'll take off. Maybe even get as far as the Dominican Republic."

This will not do at all. "So, we'll make it a surprise party," Miguel suggests.

"Hide anything from Tía Lola, are you kidding?"

But Miguel thinks it can work. After all, he and Essie were able to keep their Margaret-Henny sting operation from Tía Lola. Of course, that secret lasted less than twenty-four hours. December is a month away.

A sly look has come over Mami's face. "The only way it could work is if we were to hide the birthday party right under her nose. Say we combine Tía Lola's birthday party with the colonel's but make Tía Lola's half a surprise. Of course, we will have to be absolutely, totally . . ." Mami makes a motion of zipping up her mouth.

Not a problem for Miguel. But the same can't be said for Little Bigmouth, also known as Can't-Keep-a-Secret Juanita. After making her cross her heart and hope to die enough times to kill off a small army, Miguel fills her in on the plan. "AWESOME!" she cries out. "Oops, I'm sorry. I meant"—Juanita leans in and whispers—"awesome."

Mami talks to Víctor, who calls Carmen at the law firm where he used to work when he represented Tía Lola. Carmen digs up Tía Lola's application for staying in the United States, which includes her birth date. It turns out Tía Lola will be fifty-six years old on December 12. Víctor and his daughters are on board with the secret half of the birthday party. But they won't be telling the colonel. He'll just start fussing all over again about the half of the party that *is* for him. Meanwhile, Carmen has already asked if she and Daniel can come and bring Abuelito and Abuelita along. No one wants to miss Tía Lola's first birthday party ever, even if she is going to be fifty-six.

●●●

With so much excitement in the air (a party, two weddings, a two-in-one trip, a here-to-stay B&B), Tía Lola can't separate out the children's extra excitement over the one half of a birthday party that is going to be a surprise for her.

But a few times, she comes close to guessing the secret.

Sometimes, one of the children will let slip a remark. ("Do you think the second cake should be pink or purple?") Or Tía Lola will go on and on, adding more frills to the colonel's party (a parade, the Bridgeport school marching band leading the way; Rudy's son, Woody, doing his magic tricks), not realizing she is making a bigger party for *herself*. The children all have teeth marks on their bottom lips from biting down so hard to keep from laughing.

Planning meetings are the hardest, as Tía Lola insists on being present. After all, it was her idea to give the colonel a birthday party.

At this latest meeting, Victoria announces they are up to a hundred guests.

"A hundred?!" Tía Lola can't believe it. During their cozy evenings in the parlor, they have managed to wheedle only about forty names from the reluctant colonel.

"People have friends, Tía Lola. Look at you," Essie hints, giggling. That is precisely it: Tía Lola has a lot of friends, so the guest list is climbing. The giggles seem to be contagious. First Juanita catches them, then Cari.

Victoria eyeballs the gigglers. They are going to ruin

the surprise! "Hey, people, we need some committees here," Victoria says, trying to distract Tía Lola, who is still puzzling over the guest list. They better change the subject. Out comes Victoria's clipboard again. "I'll do the invitations and the food." Actually, all she has to do for the food is coordinate who will cook what. The party is huge. It only makes sense to have a potluck.

Essie offers to be in charge of the decorations and enlists Miguel to help her.

"Make sure you go to Estargazer," Tía Lola reminds them. Their friend's gift shop is full of neat, interesting things.

"No hay problema," Essie says, setting off a round of giggling. Tía Lola laughs along good-naturedly. The children often tease her for overusing her favorite mantra.

But the children are laughing because of a funny coincidence. For Tía Lola's surprise birthday gift, they and their parents decided to order a sign for her B&B. Lo and behold, when they walked into Stargazer's store, they learned that Tía Lola had just been in ordering the same thing! Perfect. Tía Lola will be getting exactly what she asked for. Stargazer will go ahead and fill the order according to Tía Lola's specifications. She'll set up the sign in front of the colonel's house right before the birthday party. The tricky part will be putting off Tía Lola when she tries to pay for it.

Again, Victoria has to steer the group away from hilarity or Tía Lola will get suspicious. "Juanita, how about you be in charge of entertainment."

"Sure!" Juanita loves dressing up and putting on skits.

126

"I can also do flowers. Stargazer has some really beautiful sunflowers that look so real. You know, they're her favorite flowers." Juanita gasps, realizing her slip. Oops, I'm sorry, her look says.

"*Whose* favorite flowers?" Tía Lola wants to know.

"The colonel's?" Juanita says it like she's asking a question.

"But you said '*her* favorite flowers.' "

"Did I?" Juanita smiles lamely and looks over at her partners in crime for rescue. "You must have misheard, Tía Lola. Anyhow, I meant the colonel's."

Thank goodness Cari chooses this moment to feel left out. Everybody is getting to be in a committee. "What about me?"

Tía Lola looks at her with disbelief. That she should even have to ask! "Who else can head the Utensil Committee: polishing all the silver, folding all the napkins. In fact, you sure you can manage on your own?"

Cari nods importantly. Reporting for duty, as the colonel would say.

The minute Tía Lola leaves the attic room, the children explode with laughter. Valentino barks. That reminds Cari. "What about Valentino? What can he be in charge of?"

Miguel comes up with a committee for Valentino. "You can be the head of the Distraction Committee. Like, if we're talking about Tía Lola, and you hear her coming, bark so we stop. Or if we're preparing something, distract her so we have a chance to hide any evidence. Sound like a job you can do?"

Valentino barks, You bet! The children laugh, so he barks again. The more they laugh, the more he barks. Soon Tía Lola is back at the door. "What's going on?" She looks from child to child, like she mislaid something in one of their faces and is trying to find it.

"We were, uh, just, uh, teaching, uh, Valentino . . ."

"To sing 'Happy Birthday,'" Essie rescues the flailing Juanita.

"Hmmm." Tía Lola thought she heard Valentino barking something about a surprise birthday party. She'd better bone up on her dog language. Lately, she has been feeling like her hearing is off, like she doesn't quite understand what is going on.

I am getting old, I guess, Tía Lola sighs. She will be turning fifty-six on December 12. A secret no one must know. Of course, Linda will insist on a celebration in December, since Tía Lola won't say the date. But maybe this year, with so much going on, Linda will forget, and Tía Lola's birthday can sneak by unremarked.

●●●

As October turns into November, and the weeks go by, the excitement grows. Plans are firming up. The party will be held in the colonel's house in town, also beginning to be known as Tía Lola's B&B. This time there is no danger of the invitations being altered. Odette and Henny are actually helping fill them out. Included in each invite is a note explaining that half of the party is a big surprise for Tía Lola, who will be turning fifty-six three days after the colonel. The town is bursting at the seams to keep its secret.

Even the colonel is getting into the spirit of the upcoming party, which, of course, he thinks is only for him. Everyone he loves will be gathered together under one roof. "It'll be like attending my own funeral, and getting to enjoy it."

"Oh, please don't say that, Colonel Charlebois," Victoria pleads with the old man. She hates funerals, especially for those she loves.

Essie is more direct. "You better not die on us, Colonel, or we'll kill you."

Meanwhile, Tía Lola is losing steam. Everywhere she goes, conversation stops, then starts again, everyone politely including her. But Tía Lola can tell that they aren't truly glad to see her.

When she brings up Colonel Charlebois's party, only weeks away, she can't help noticing people exchanging glances. Maybe Victoria forgot to invite them?

But Victoria confirms that those people got invitations. "Is something wrong, Tía Lola?" the eldest Sword asks. Her usually happy friend has been looking uncharacteristically sad.

Tía Lola shakes her head. But she doesn't add her usual perky mantra, *"No hay problema."* She wouldn't want to worry the kind Victoria, but lately she has been wondering if maybe the town is getting tired of her. Maybe her B&B isn't such a good idea. And now she has gone and ordered a sign! Every time she tries to pay for it, her friend tells her not to worry about it yet. It's almost as if Stargazer were hoping that Tía Lola would just forget about starting a B&B and go back to being a stay-at-home *tía* instead.

The final straw comes one Saturday afternoon, a week before the party. Tía Lola is running some errands downtown and decides to drop in on her old friend Rudy. The door to Amigos Café is locked, which is strange, but it is that lull after lunch and before dinner.

Tía Lola goes to knock on the big picture window in case Rudy is out back. And what a surprise: right there in plain sight are all the kids, and Linda and Víctor, sitting around a table with Rudy. On every face is an unmistakable look of Oh no, it's her! Even the children, who have begged her to stay, now want her to go away.

Rudy comes to the door and doesn't invite her in. "I'm, uh, really busy, um, with, um, the dinner menu," he offers as an excuse. He seems to have forgotten that he was just sitting around a table, chatting with a bunch of friends.

"*No hay problema,*" Tía Lola says quietly, giving everyone a wistful little wave. Then she turns and walks down the block, head down, spirits low.

Ahead looms the colonel's house with its magnificent maple tree, now looking so bereft and leafless. Its spindly branches seem like fingers pointing at her. Go back to where you came from! Tía Lola can take a hint. When the family heads down for Christmas to visit the relatives, she will announce her decision. "It's time for me to stay in my own country." *Adiós* and goodbye to Tía Lola's B&B.

●●●

"I think we just hurt her feelings big-time." Victoria looks pained herself. She is ready to run after Tía Lola and fess up, even if Tía Lola ends up hightailing it out of town.

"We'll tie her down." Essie is always one to milk any moment for its last drop of drama. "We'll give her Knock-Me-Out Tea and keep her asleep until Saturday."

"That's not funny," her older sister tells her.

"I haven't seen Tía Lola look that sad in ages." Linda is starting to regret the whole idea of a surprise party. "I don't know. Maybe we should just tell her the truth."

"But we're so close—only a week longer," Rudy points out.

And yet who can bear to have Tía Lola suffering for a whole day, much less a week? Certainly not Cari. "Why don't we just give her her surprise party now?"

"Now? But how can we?" All of Victoria's organization will go out the window. "We can't start calling people. I mean, they have to plan and make their recipes."

But Víctor has started nodding in Cari's direction. "You know, Caridad Espada, I think you've come up with a great solution. Seriously. I'll go pick up a cake. Get a few party items at Stargazer's. We can do the surprise part of Tía Lola's party now, just us. We'll ask her to forgive us, and promise never to give her a *surprise* party again. Which completely absolves us from giving her a birthday party next Saturday, because it won't technically be a *surprise* anymore." A tricky argument. All those years of legal training have not been for nothing.

" 'All's well that ends well,' we'll tell her," Rudy says, laughing. They all know how much Tía Lola loves a good saying.

They go into high gear. Rudy has a cake on hand he can quickly decorate. Linda and Victoria head for the grocery store to pick up some drinks and groceries for rice and beans and chicken, Tía Lola's favorite meal. Víctor runs down to Stargazer's with Essie and Juanita and Cari.

Meanwhile, Miguel has been drafted by Valentino's Distraction Committee to make sure Tía Lola stays at the colonel's. She might decide to slip away and visit one of her many friends—although as sad as she looked when she turned away from Amigos Café, Miguel doubts it.

They find Tía Lola in the backyard, sitting on the very bench where Henny had her rendezvous with her aunt Margaret. It is a mild, early-winter afternoon, but still chilly enough that Miguel is surprised that his aunt should linger outdoors. She hasn't even bothered to tie her lucky yellow scarf around her neck. It just hangs over her shoulders like every drop of luck has drained out of it. "Aren't you cold, Tía Lola?" he asks her.

Tía Lola shakes her head. Not as cold as she felt looking into Amigos Café and seeing the frosty looks her *familia* gave her. But Tía Lola would never say so. She would not want to hurt her nephew. He is growing up. He doesn't need his old aunt around anymore. This is the natural course of life. He shouldn't be made to feel bad about it.

Miguel isn't used to seeing Tía Lola sad. She's usually the one lifting his spirits. He tries to recall what she does when he is feeling low. One thing she always tries is some wise saying. "You know, Tía Lola, every cloud has a silver lining."

Tía Lola scans the overcast sky. "They do?" So Miguel has to explain that clouds don't really have silver linings.

132

It's just a way of saying that there's some good in everything.

"Is that so?" Tía Lola sounds doubtful.

Well, that saying didn't work. Miguel glances desper-
ately at Valentino: It's your turn, President of the Distraction Committee. You try to make Tía Lola smile.

But Valentino flashes Miguel a desperate look back. He
can't think of anything either. Miguel gives it another try:
"Tía Lola, if you could make a wish right this minute,
what would make you happiest of all?"

Tía Lola has been acting very distant, as if her thoughts
are far away, maybe in the Dominican Republic. But suddenly she is back, surprised by her nephew's question.
"Why . . . I suppose I would wish to be surrounded by
the people I love. And to feel," she adds, sighing, "that they
love me and want me there."

Just then, they hear voices inside the house, calling.
Essie's head pops out the back door. "They're out here,"
she hollers over her shoulder.

Tía Lola stands up, brushing the wrinkles out of her
skirt, straightening her yellow scarf. She actually is feeling
better. "Thank you for asking, Miguel."

"*No hay problema,* Tía Lola. By the way, can I borrow
your lucky scarf a moment?"

Tía Lola looks perplexed. "Of course," she says, slipping it off. A lot of luck it's brought her in the last few
weeks! "But what do you want it for?"

"It's a surprise. Now, turn around and let me blind-
fold you."

It's as if Miguel just poured water on a wilting plant. Tía Lola perks right up, smiling ear to ear as her nephew blindfolds her. Then, with Valentino on the other side, Miguel leads his aunt into the house, through the kitchen to the dining room, and unties her scarf.

Tía Lola blinks. She can't believe her eyes. All around her are the people she loves, holding purple balloons and wearing party hats. "Surprise! *¡Sorpresa!*" they cry out, and break into the birthday song. On the table sits a white cake with one candle and purple letters spelling out FELIZ CUMPLEAÑOS, TÍA LOLA. WE LOVE YOU.

"Make a wish," they remind her before she blows out the candle.

"I don't need to," Tía Lola says, winking at Miguel. "My wish has already come true."

la ñapa

How Tía Lola Ended Up Starting Over

Do you remember all the way back to the first Tía Lola book, *How Tía Lola Came to ~~Visit~~ Stay,* where Miguel learned about *ñapas*? He and his family were flying down to the Dominican Republic for Christmas (just as he and his new *familia* will be doing in a few weeks). Tía Lola was telling him and Juanita about customs in her native country. "Don't forget to ask for your *ñapa* when you go to the market." A *ñapa,* she went on to explain, is that little extra that comes at the end.

You buy a dozen mangoes, and then, for your *ñapa,* you get one more. Or you order a double ice cream cone, and you get a little added scoop as your *ñapa.* Or it's time to come in at night. You can ask for your *ñapa,* just five more minutes to try to tie up the soccer game.

It also works in books. The last chapter of the last book on Tía Lola has come to an end. Here is a *ñapa* before Tía Lola says *adiós* to all our friends.

●●●

After surprising Tía Lola with her cake, it's time for her party. Víctor makes a fire; Valentino fetches her slippers; Cari and Juanita each take a foot to massage.

They eat around the fire, saving the cake for last. Of course, they insist on singing another round of "Happy Birthday."

Tía Lola comes clean. "You know, it's not really my birthday today."

"We know, Tía Lola. It's December twelfth." Juanita grins like a TV contestant with the right answer. "You're going to be fifty-six."

Tía Lola is shocked. How on earth did they find out?

Víctor explains how Tía Lola's birth date was on her application to stay in the USA. "Carmen looked it up for us."

"You forgive us, Tía Lola?" Victoria pleads for them all.

"Forgive you for what?"

"That we threw you a surprise birthday party." Cari wishes Papa would remind everyone that it was her idea.

"How can I be upset when you did something out of love?" Tía Lola shakes her head. "Don't you know what they say, *Buenas razones cautivan los corazones*?" Good intentions win hearts. Miguel and Juanita learned that saying in Tía Lola's second book. She was afraid to come teach Spanish at their school, thinking she wasn't smart enough.

So Miguel and Juanita made up a story about it being Bring a Special Person to School Day. Tía Lola forgave them for tricking her, because they acted out of good intentions. They didn't want her to feel lonely all by herself at home all day long.

"But I still don't get why you'd keep your birthday a secret." Essie would never in a zillion years hide her birthday from anybody.

Tía Lola sighs, glancing over at Linda, who understands. Tía Lola has been hiding her birthday all her life so as not to cause her niece any expense or bother.

"But those hard days are over, Tía Lola," Linda says in a tender voice. "We're not rich, Tía Lola, but we have enough now to celebrate the people we love." And then Mami tells Tía Lola the whole truth: the big party next weekend will also be for her.

"But you can't run away, Tía Lola!" Essie warns. "Or we'll kill you."

Run away? How can she? Tía Lola is still responsible for the colonel's half of the birthday party next Saturday.

Miguel has been devouring his cake, sharing a dollop of frosting with the president of the Distraction Committee. "How about my *ñapa,* Tía Lola?" he says, holding up his empty plate. This prompts Cari to ask what a nappy is—she thought it was a diaper. Miguel explains, and soon all the kids are clamoring for their *ñapas,* until the cake is gone.

Except for one lone candle sitting among crumbs on the platter. No one can be enticed to take it for future use. The whole *familia,* including Tía Lola, have had their fill of making wishes. Wishes can be risky, they can backfire on you. But *ñapas* are a sure bet. All you are asking for is a little bit more of what has already proved to be a good thing. Another slice of excellent cake. A few more pages of a story before it finally comes to an end.

●●●

Saturday afternoon, a week later. The house is bustling with activity. A crew is rearranging the furniture: pushing the dining-room table to one side and adding several card tables for the buffet to be laid out. A large picnic basket sits at one end holding the utensils: napkins wrapped around gleaming silver forks and knives.

Outside, snow is beginning to fall. Christmas is coming in less than two weeks. All down Main Street, the lampposts are strung with holiday lights, and every shop window has a Santa or a Christmas tree. At the library, with its four columns sporting red bows, the librarian turns the OPEN sign around to CLOSED at the door.

This evening, the shops are all closing early. Everyone is rushing home to change and put the finishing touches on their potluck contributions for the big party at Tía Lola's B&B. Salads and soups, homemade breads and casseroles galore. The desserts look like beauty contestants, vying to outshine each other, some frothy with icing, others exotically dark and chocolatey, still others studded with bits of candied fruit like jewels. They all deserve crowns.

Out in the snowy driveway in front of Colonel Charlebois's house, Stargazer and her friends are unloading Tía Lola's gift from the back of Rudy's pickup. Earlier, two posts were driven into the ground, each with a slot for holding the sign in place. Tía Lola had looked up from scrubbing a pot in the kitchen. "What is that hammering?" Miguel managed to convince his aunt that the banging was just the sound of furniture being pushed to one side of the parlor to make room for all their guests.

Tía Lola is hurriedly finishing up her cooking to free up the oven for warming the guests' contributions when they come. But just in case she should decide to wander toward the front of the house, the Distraction Committee has devised an alarm system: Miguel is posted by the door, blocking the way out of the kitchen. Behind him lies Valentino, like a speed bump. If all else fails, Miguel will stall, Valentino will bark, and Essie will open the front parlor window and holler: DUCK!

Out front, the sign is finally in place, a white sheet draped over it. As the snow accumulates on top, the surprise gift starts looking like a body waiting to be buried.

Or so Essie comments to the colonel as they stand guard by the parlor window.

"So, my party will be a funeral after all. Just not my own, thank God." The colonel chuckles, Essie giggles, and soon they are both laughing hysterically.

Back in the kitchen, Tía Lola is waiting for her *pastelón,* a tasty chicken casserole, to come out of the oven. She cleans her hands on her apron and heads toward the front of the house.

Miguel blocks her passage. "Where are you going, Tía Lola?"

"What do you mean, where am I going? To check on the *coronel*, of course."

"The colonel is fine," Miguel says quickly. "Essie's with him."

"That is what I am worried about," Tía Lola says, stepping over her favorite *mascota*. Mix Essie with the colonel and you have the ingredients for trouble. But no sooner is Tía Lola halfway down the hall than Valentino has a major barking meltdown. Tía Lola turns her attention to the dog, but just then the phone rings. It's one of the guests. They might be a little late on account of the snow has really started coming down. By the time Tía Lola hangs up and heads for the parlor, the oven timer is beeping. Her casserole is done.

The snow keeps falling. It's as if someone has shaken a snow globe, at the center of which sits a small town full of happy people. From the far corners of their little world they are coming together to celebrate two legends: An old colonel who spent his life serving in the army but finally came back to his hometown to serve in whatever way he can. And then, another legendary figure: a remarkable, lively lady from the Dominican Republic who in less than two years has brought this community together.

They drive in from the countryside: the Magoons, all five of them, with a wheelchair covered with a tarp in back; Tom and Becky, the sheep farmers, in fresh coveralls, comb marks still showing in their wet hair; Margaret and Odette and Henny, each bearing a recipe Margaret wanted to try out from a tribe she has studied. "Don't worry," she assures the children. "No tarantulas or locusts or human flesh among the ingredients." She winks at Miguel, who recently asked her if she'd ever eaten a human being. "Not on purpose," she replied disconcertingly.

Last night, to avoid the predicted snowfall, Papi and Carmen drove up from New York City with Abuelito and Abuelita. Ming was going to come, but her parents were afraid that with the bad weather, they might be stranded in Vermont forever. "Which would make me totally happy," Ming confessed to Juanita over the phone. She was ready to run away, but Juanita talked her out of it.

As the guests start arriving, Tía Lola greets them at the door. *"¡Sorpresa!"* she cries, totally surprising *them.* So, Tía Lola found out about her party after all.

"We gave her her surprise last week. It was my idea," Cari adds because Papa never remembers to say so.

"Tía Lola, we do have one last surprise," Miguel announces. Earlier, the children voted him to be their spokesperson, maybe to make up for the fact that he will soon be the only boy in their combined *familia.* Miguel has climbed up to the landing on the stairs. It's the only way to get the attention of this noisy congregation. "It's your surprise birthday gift. But you have to go outside to see it."

"A parade?" Tía Lola guesses. But how can that be? The school already decided against a parade for the colonel. The marching band might catch pneumonia.

"I'm not telling. It's a surprise, and not a surprise," Miguel says mysteriously.

Now Tía Lola is really intrigued. These children are talking in riddles, inventing adventures, coming up with fun ideas. She has taught them well. Last summer, in her third book, they learned that the power was inside them. And how! They can run magic circles around her now.

Tía Lola bundles up in her jacket, tying her yellow scarf around her neck. It did not fail her after all. Through the thick and thin of four books, it has been her lucky charm. Outside, the crowd gathers around a mysterious white mound that has appeared on the front lawn. So that's why Miguel and Valentino were trying to keep her in the back of the house!

The snow keeps falling. The outdoor lights illuminate the flakes coming down like confetti thrown at a wedding or like ticker tape in a parade. It's as if Vermont is giving Tía Lola the parade she wanted for the colonel after all. By morning there will be enough snow for a snowman.

"Hooray for Tía Lola! Hooray for the colonel!" the guests cheer.

"Happy birthday, Tía Lola. This is from all of us." Miguel gestures toward the mystery gift, then toward Juanita and the Swords, and their various parents and parents-to-be.

"TA-RUM!" Essie says, impersonating a trumpet. Miguel lifts the sheet; snow flies every which way.

The sign reads TÍA LOLA'S C&C&C.

"Ah!" Tía Lola exclaims. She looks over nervously at Stargazer, as if to say, Don't breathe a word about the other sign that I ordered and ruin their surprise. *"¡Perfecto!"*

It is? The kids can't believe it. Spacey Stargazer must

have messed up and carved the wrong letters. "It's supposed to say '*B&B*,'" Essie points out.

Stargazer lifts up her mittened hands. "That's what I thought, too. But I double-checked with Tía Lola. And that's what she wanted." Stargazer goes on to tell the story of the funny coincidence. "This is the sign you ordered, Tía Lola, but it's their gift. That's why I couldn't let you pay for it."

"All's well," Rudy begins, and everyone chimes in, "that ends well."

But wait. Essie still doesn't get it. "What *is* a C&C&C?"

"My very own Spanish B&B!" Tía Lola lifts her arms, introducing her creation to the world. As her last book is coming to an end, she is happy to be starting over on a new adventure. "Tía Lola's *Cama* & *Comida* & *Cariño*. Bed and food and most important, *cariño*!" By now, the whole town is practically bilingual, so everyone knows that *"cariño"* means "love."

In the years to come, people will try to find this charming establishment in a friendly little town in rural Vermont. They will drive around in the autumn, looking for the magnificent maple in the front yard; and in the winter, for the snowman with a yellow scarf and a plastic sword in his hand. The spring will bring them to the surrounding woods to hike; and the summer, to nearby lakes and sleepaway camps. Season after season, they will try to find Tía Lola's C&C&C, only to give up until their next trip to Vermont.

But even if they program their GPS and drive around

for days, they won't find what they are looking for. Except for the few who climb the steps to the small library on Main Street, the one with columns that looks like a monument celebrating some important person or deed. Inside, an important activity is indeed going on: people are reading, old people and teenagers, mommas and *mamis, papis* and papas and dads, *tíos* and *tías,* uncles and aunts, *abuelitos* and grandparents. Down in the basement, with a whole floor to themselves, little kids are reading alone on pillows in cozy corners, or reading to each other in small groups of two or four, or lying inside an old-fashioned claw-foot bathtub reading to the stuffed animals.

Just inside the basement door, shelved under *A,* they will find the Tía Lola books. Maybe they'll start with the first one, or maybe the third, then backtrack to the second and first, but eventually they will arrive at Tía Lola's C&C&C. By then, of course, the house will be painted purple with magenta shutters, and the sign up front will be decked on either side with bushes pruned in the shapes of hearts or parrots or flamingos. Upstairs, their *camas* will be turned down, and in the kitchen, their *comidas* will be warming in the oven. Their hearts will fill with *cariño,* so much so that they will have a hard time leaving.

But by then, they will know that they can always come back. All they have to do is open one of her books, without making a reservation or calling in advance. There is always a vacancy at Tía Lola's C&C&C, no matter how many guests flock here.

So if you see people walking around, looking a little lost or scratching their heads and sighing, or showing any of the telltale signs that they are still searching for something they can't quite put into words, please tell them where to go. It might not be in a Tía Lola book, but inside one of the many books on the shelves of their libraries, surely they will find what they are looking for.

acknowledgments

Just as Tía Lola
loves to invite guests
to her B&B,
I am inviting
each of you
who helped me write this book
to a free weekend
at Tía Lola's C&C&C:

Weybridge Elementary School

Roberto Veguez

Lyn Tavares

Susan Bergholz

Erin Clarke

Bill Eichner

Brian Goodwin

Katherine Branch

Erica Stahler

The Snells at Tourterelle

The Middlebury College Men's and Women's
Water Polo Teams

Brad Nadeau (who deserves a season's worth
of weekends)

Hannah and Missy Williams (who helped me
prove a point)

Muchas gracias and many thanks to all of you
and to la Virgencita de la Altagracia.